AN UNSAVORY MESS

Tyora Moody

Tymm Publishing
Columbia, SC

An Unsavory Mess
A Eugeena Patterson Mystery, Book 5

Copyright © 2021 by Tyora Moody

Published by Tymm Publishing LLC
PO Box 8384
1600 Assembly St
Columbia, SC 29202
www.tymmpublishing.com

Cover Design: TywebbinCreations.com
Copy Editing/Proofreading: Felicia Murrell

For our struggle is not against flesh and blood, but against the rulers, against the authorities, against the powers of this dark world and against the spiritual forces of evil in the heavenly realms (Ephesians 6:12, NIV).

Acknowledgements

Hello reader, thank you for picking up book number five from this series. I hope you find each mystery better than the last with Eugeena proving life after retirement can indeed be an adventure. I want to thank a few people who helped me shape this current story you're about to read.

I want to thank my editor, Felicia Murrell for lending her eyes to this latest adventure. Your ability to catch details that I always miss is very valuable to my writing process and helps make the story shine.

I want to thank my dad for playing those records when I was a child. Who knew those same 70s hits would immediately come to mind as I started to wander back in time imagining life as a teenager for Eugeena.

As always, thanks to my mom whose advice and encouragement helped me work out some kinks as I wrote this book.

I want to acknowledge the success of this series has been amplified by the talented Sharell Palmer. I'm so happy she remains the narrator for the audiobook versions.

I finished this book at what I hope is the tail end of the pandemic. I'm looking forward to getting back out there to meet with readers in person. In the meantime, I've enjoyed and want to express my thanks to the book clubs who met with me virtually to discuss Eugeena's books. I hope as this series continues that some loose ends have started to come together from earlier books in the series. I appreciate the passionate responses I've received about Eugeena and the other cast of characters.

I also want to give a shoutout to members of the Tyora

Moody VIP Readers Facebook Group especially Marsha Cecil, Rosemary Ross, Rena Anderson, Lavern Aslam, and Arlena Gordon Dean.

I'm truly grateful to God for giving me a love for storytelling as a reader and a writer. I'm humbled and amazed with how much I love writing this character and how Sugar Creek feels like home. There are so many times when I find myself laughing out loud, moved to tears or even thinking how close these fictional situations seem to parallel my own personal experiences.

Cast of Characters

Sugar Creek is a fictional neighborhood in Charleston, South Carolina. In An Unsavory Mess, readers will find many familiar supporting characters from previous Eugeena Patterson mysteries. Just in case you need a reminder of who is who, refer to this list below. I promise that any character introduced from the Sugar Creek neighborhood has something to contribute to the story. I hope you enjoy dropping by the neighborhood for a visit. Ms. Eugeena appreciates you joining the adventure.

Eugeena's Family

Amos Jones (Eugeena's second husband, retired homicide detective)

Ralph Patterson, Jr. (oldest son married to Judy, twin boys, Jacob and Joseph, girl, Jasmine)

Cedric Patterson (son married to Carmen Alpine-Patterson)

Leesa Patterson (daughter, single, two children, Kisha and Tyric)

Briana Jones (Amos' youngest daughter; lives in old family home next door)

Cora Gibson (aunt closest in age to Eugeena)

Esther Gibson (oldest living aunt)

Porgy (the family dog, a Corgi)

Recurring Characters from the Series

Detective Sarah Wilkes

Detective Chris Black (Leesa's boyfriend, Tyric's father, new to Charleston PD)

Annie Mae Brown (Missionary Baptist Church, volunteer)

Willie Mae Brown (Missionary Baptist Church, volunteer)

Rosemary Gladstone (Eugeena's longtime friend and high school classmate)

Michelle Gladstone (Rosemary's daughter and Amani's mom)

Amani Gladstone (precocious student; Rosemary's granddaughter)

Louise Hopkins (Eugeena's next door neighbor)

Jocelyn "Joss" Miller (Louise's granddaughter)

Fay Everett (Eugeena's former student, Owner of Sugar Creek Cafe)

Chapter 1

I looked good! Felt like a million bucks and that didn't happen too often for a sistah like me. I'd had some bad days for the past few months. Experiencing a good day for a change lifted my spirits.

I couldn't remember the last time I dressed up in formal clothes. Tonight, I wore a burgundy dress with sequins embroidered on the front. Now I still struggled with my weight, so my brand-new Spanx had me feeling younger. I almost forgot I'd been wearing it, and that alone was enough to make me smile.

What really had me grinning like a schoolgirl was the man in front of me.

Amos Jones, my husband.

Still newlyweds, we married eight months ago, and despite some unforeseeable incidents, we continued to enjoy each other's company. That's all that mattered. Right now, we danced like we were teenagers again to "Fire" by the Ohio Players. I believe it was the first time we'd partied since our wedding.

I have to thank my bestie, Rosemary Gladstone, who berated me a few weeks ago about my desire to skip yet another high school reunion. Still grieving for my first husband, I avoided the fortieth class reunion. The reason for I skipped the others, I couldn't recall. This was the first time Rosemary had chaired the reunion committee, so the least I could do was support her. The high school classmate who had previously kept the tradition sadly passed away and someone else had to pick up the reins.

Rosemary had been the manager of events at the Charleston Place Hotel for years. Since she oversaw bookings at the hotel all the time, it was quite easy for her to reserve the ballroom for our forty-fifth reunion. The grand and historical building offered an elegant setting. I did not know where Rosemary found the disco balls, but the glittering lights were perfect and hypnotized me back into time.

The DJ changed to a more mellow song which was fine by me. My body reminded me I was sixty-two. I smiled and swayed to "Ain't Nothing Like the Real Thing." Most people are used to hearing the version by Marvin Gaye and Tammi Terrell, but I had a sweet spot for the version sung by Aretha Franklin. Her voice touched my soul.

Amos did a shuffle and winked at me. "May I have this dance?"

"Absolutely." I placed my arm around his shoulder, oblivious to everyone around us.

I was truly grateful for how much I loved this man.

Amos had been by my side for quite a few years before we were hitched. Neighbors and both widows, it seemed like a likely pairing for a second time down the altar. I think what really brought us together was the fact that I had a tendency to stick my nose into places that often involved a dead body. Amos, being a former homicide detective, always came to my rescue.

The last time, I really got into hot water. Though my

purpose was to clear Amos' daughter from being a prime suspect in a murder, I was surprised by the actual murderer. So I have since promised my family there would be no more amateur sleuth adventures from me. I felt good about making that promise. In all honesty, the last incident scared me to pieces. I couldn't sleep for weeks. Sometimes I still woke Amos up after having a nightmare.

The song changed over to "Can't Get Enough of Your Love." I looked at Amos. "Now I love some Barry White, but my feet have had enough."

He chuckled. "I'm glad we attended your reunion tonight."

"Me too. I didn't think showing up at my forty-fifth high school reunion would be so much fun. Or maybe I need to get out more, Mr. Jones."

Amos threw his head back and laughed. "We are retired. There's no reason we can't do a lot more. I told you we could even travel if you want."

The thought had occurred to me a few times; I hadn't taken a vacation in a long time. Before we walked back to our table, Amos and I helped ourselves to a second plate from the serving table. Dancing worked up an appetite. The reunion had been catered by the local restaurant, the Chicken Shack. There were an array of wings, both fried and roasted arranged on large platters. Tiny cups of sauce like ranch, honey mustard and barbecue were nearby. The addition of a honey flavored biscuit and iced tea to my plate had me feeling like I was walking on a cloud.

Dancing and eating good food. I couldn't have asked for a better Saturday night.

While Amos and I munched, I took another moment to look around at my classmates. We were all in our early sixties, but everyone for the most part was looking good. I caught sight of Rosemary across the room.

Now Rosemary was about my size, but unlike me, she was still a beauty. I'd never been the beauty queen type, but Rosemary had won many competitions in her day. There weren't many times, except during her downtime at home, when her face wasn't flawlessly made up. She kept her hair dyed honey blond, making sure no gray hair ever appeared.

She wore her favorite color tonight. The mauve dress hung slightly off one of Rosemary's shoulders and accentuated her curves. Somehow, she defied her age, appearing younger than the rest of us.

Right now my friend's caramel face appeared mottled with red marks on her cheeks and she was glaring at something or someone across the room.

Amos asked, "Something wrong?"

"I don't know, but Rosemary is looking upset. That's not like her. She's the most jovial person I know. Let me see what's going on. I know she was stressed about coordinating this reunion, but she's done a fabulous job."

"I agree. Let's go over and see if she needs our help with anything."

That's my Amos. Who knew a man could be so thoughtful.

As I approached, I watched Rosemary wipe her eyes.

Who has my sistahfriend crying?

Now, I knew this was serious. Rosemary was like me. We had to be really angry and upset for you to make us cry. I rushed over. "Rosemary, what's wrong?"

She turned and looked at me. "You will know in a second; she's on her way over here. She started trouble as soon as she walked in the door."

"What?" I spun around, and then sucked in a breath. "What's she doing here? I thought she didn't RSVP."

Rosemary cleared her throat. "She told me herself that she would never come to one of these if I coordinated it. She said Pauline was the best."

Pauline Jackson had died a few years back. The former class president faithfully coordinated reunions and even cruise trips for members of our class. She was truly a force to be reckoned with until cancer got to her. I'd heard she was diagnosed before the last reunion, but kept the party going regardless. Pauline was a dear, but her best friend was hell on wheels or in this case tonight, hell on heels.

As she marched our way, Georgia Hayes' sourpuss face was on full display. This was her standard 'I don't like this at all and I'm going to tell you so' face. One would think she had grown up after forty-five years. But Georgia had always been a petty person, always looking for trouble. And even though she had the looks, she seemed to be really insecure, especially around other pretty females like Rosemary.

My only real run-in with Georgia had to do with knowing how much she really wanted Ralph Patterson in high school. She was Ralph's girlfriend briefly during high school, probably right before he started courting me. When everyone found out about my pregnancy, I recall Georgia having the meanest reaction. She had the nerve to accuse me of holding Ralph back with my pregnancy. The crazy thing, for many years after I'd married Ralph, I believed her. Other than this ancient history, I rarely ran into Georgia, even though we both lived in Charleston.

Now Rosemary and Georgia's clashes were intense. Both considered the prettiest girls in our class, their rivalry drew attention school-wide. Rosemary kept her good

Christian girl demeanor while Georgia's reputation strayed a bit more risqué with the boys. Both women competed for everything, including homecoming queen, prom queen, and even captain of the cheerleading squad.

I steeled myself as the woman approached, preparing for whatever was about to happen.

Georgia had always been a slim woman, and even now in her early sixties, she remained slim. And although she tried to cover it with makeup, I could see age had taken a toll on her. Tonight, she wore a sequined silver dress with matching heels. The outfit would have been cute on a much younger woman with curves.

The dress hung like an expensive sack of potatoes on Georgia.

She launched into her tirade. "Did you really have to have the reunion in this fancy place? Are you too good for the high school gym?"

Rosemary looked at her, fist balled. "I tried to have it at the high school, but there are lots of events going on this month. I didn't want to risk losing the opportunity. Besides, for our age group, the ballroom presents a more comfortable environment. A lot of our classmates live out of town and it's easier for them to be near their hotel rooms. The high school is nowhere near any kind of convenience."

Georgia waved her hand as if knocking away a fly. "Oh, you just want to make sure everything goes your way as you did in high school."

Rosemary rolled her eyes. "Really, Georgia, why are you being so dramatic? Just enjoy yourself. Pauline would have loved this."

"How would you know? You weren't friends."

Rosemary sighed. "Pauline and I got along just fine. In

fact, the year before she coordinated the Bahamas cruise, she reached out to me about the ballroom. But it was booked."

Georgia's expression didn't change, but the mention of her friend seemed to make her grow angrier. "I don't believe you. Pauline would have mentioned it to me."

I looked back and forth from Rosemary to Georgia thinking we all might be in our sixties, but it felt like something had suddenly sucked us back in time.

So, like long ago, I added my two cents. "Look, Rosemary has done a marvelous job with the reunion. Everyone is enjoying themselves. What's your problem, Georgia?"

Wouldn't you know, at that very moment, the DJ suddenly had nothing else to play. The sound of my sharp words paralyzed as if someone had turned a spotlight on me. I peered around at the crowd as they stared back at me. The eerie quiet replaced the party mood with something more malevolent that made my skin crawl.

Now I wished I'd stayed home.

Chapter 2

It could have just been my sudden paranoia, but I envisioned sparks in my classmates' eyes. Like they were hungry for a good old-fashioned catfight. When I caught Amos' eye, I really started cringing.

I was having such a good time!

Amos had his arms up in a gesture of pure confusion. I waved at him and gave him my-everything-is going-to-be-okay smile. He returned my smile with his yeah-right look. The man knew three women arguing, one of them being his wife, was trouble in the making.

From across the room, a man's voice boomed. "DJ, what happened to the music?" Thank goodness some other classmates chimed in.

Soon, "The Hustle" blasted from the speakers.

How appropriate!

Georgia needed to hustle her behind out of this building. Why couldn't she leave her petty spirit at home?

At that moment, Jimmy Hayes walked over and stood behind Georgia. Jimmy was Georgia's high school sweetheart, whom she later married. Not too long after I had my first child, Georgia had her own baby. She and Jimmy married young, too, and were now divorced.

Jimmy crossed his enormous arms like he was a bouncer. "Georgia, what are you doing?"

That's when I realized the voice I'd heard chastising the DJ belonged to him.

Georgia rolled her eyes so dramatically the whites of her eyes displayed for a split second too long. She sucked on her teeth and looked even more contrite. "Jimmy, don't come over here bothering me. I have something to say and I'm going to say it."

I watched as Jimmy lifted his eyes to the ceiling as if he wanted God to come down and strike his ex-wife.

Either she was oblivious or she didn't care. I was betting on the latter.

Georgia lifted her finger as if she was about to scold disobedient children. "My dear friend Pauline must be turning over in her grave about this bougie event called a reunion."

Rosemary's caramel skin turned even redder around the cheeks. "Seriously, Georgia, I would have thought you'd learned the art of having some class by now. I believe you just like being mean for no reason."

My mouth dropped open, not because I didn't agree with my friend; it surprised me she'd said that to Georgia's face. Rosemary had always been the diplomatic one.

My friend blinked a few times as her own words hit her. She attempted to appease Georgia. "Some of our classmates are not here anymore. We should be grateful for the opportunity, don't you think? I think I did the best I could, and I didn't do it alone. We had a fabulous committee, including some of the same people who worked with Pauline for past reunions. Unlike you, I think we made her proud that we're keeping the reunion going."

Georgia yelped. "It was supposed to be me doing all of this. Pauline was my friend."

Rosemary glanced at me. "I'm sorry, Georgia. Why didn't you say anything when I reached out to you? You seemed uninterested."

"Whatever! This is just like it was in high school. Nothing has changed." She gulped in air as if she was on the verge of hyperventilating. "Maybe I should be grateful that nothing has changed. Everything else has." Georgia stormed off, leaving Rosemary and me shaking our heads.

Jimmy looked at us apologetically. "I'm sorry. There is no excuse for her being this way, but she has been having a hard time lately, especially after losing Pauline. I will go see if I can talk to her."

I raised an eyebrow. I'd never understood what Jimmy saw in Georgia, but I was glad someone cared enough to talk sense into her, though I doubted he could.

Amos tapped me on the shoulder. "What was that about?"

I shook my head. "That was Georgia. She was not the friendliest to me and especially Rosemary. I believe she was jealous then and still jealous now."

Amos shook his head. "Forty-five years is a long time to hold a grudge."

"You're right."

I needed to visit the ladies' room and asked Rosemary to tagalong. Once inside the sparkling bathroom, I did a check of the stalls before selecting one. Rosemary and I met at the sinks.

She sighed. "I don't get it. If she wanted to coordinate this reunion, why didn't she start on it sooner? I didn't get the call for help until late spring and I've had to scramble to pull this all together."

I grabbed paper towels from the basket to dry my hands. "I know. You've done a great job. It seems like Georgia still has some old animosities."

Rosemary held her hand to her head. "I've never had a grudge. I still don't. Eugeena, you know I try to get along with everybody."

"Yes, you do."

The door to the bathroom opened, and in the mirror, I glimpsed Claudia Benson and Sharise Long. Now, these two ladies were about as opposite as two people could be.

Claudia was tall and slim. She'd also been on the cheerleading squad in high school. Claudia was one of those women who looked better as they aged. Tonight she wore a simple black dress which on someone else might have looked like funeral wear, but Claudia pulled it off elegantly.

Sharise, like me, had always been a bit on the pudgy side. Now in her sixties, she had grown even rounder. She'd always had a cute face and remained the shortest member of our class. Sharise waddled over towards the sink, her face grim.

Though everyone knew each other in our class of fifty-four students, there were always people who congregated toward each other. I knew why.

Georgia was enemy number one to quite a few people in our class, but Pauline, Claudia and Sharise were her constant companions.

I wouldn't call them friends; I recalled Georgia bullying both Claudia and Sharise when we were younger.

Claudia peered in the mirror, smoothing down her perfectly arched eyebrow with her fingers. "Are you two okay? Everyone heard Georgia going off."

Sharise chimed in. "That woman never had any good sense. Someone needs to put her in her place."

Claudia looked over her shoulder. "I believe Jimmy went after her to talk some sense into her. That man, bless his heart, he will never stop loving that woman even though she's done him so wrong."

I nodded. "We all need someone who cares about us. I thought all of you were friends."

Sharise balked. "Nope, not for a while for me. Claudia still puts up with her."

Claudia crossed her arms. "She's had a rough time. I try to check on her now and then. Last I talked to her, she wasn't planning on coming tonight."

Rosemary shook her head. "She apparently didn't feel it was my place to take over Pauline's role."

Claudia turned to Rosemary. "Don't pay attention to her. Georgia couldn't have pulled this off. You have done a wonderful job and we are all having a good time. I didn't need to, but I got a room upstairs for the evening. This hotel is the perfect getaway, and I love the view of historic downtown Charleston. I lived here all my life but sometimes you can lose sight of all the history here."

I watched as Rosemary teared up over the comments. She sniffled. "Thank you, Claudia. I'm glad you could get away. I have done that myself."

Sharise smiled. "I had a good time too, Rosemary. This may have been the best reunion yet."

I looked in the mirror, catching Rosemary's eyes. "See, you can't let Georgia ruin this for you. You pulled this together in record time and even got me to attend."

We all left the ladies' room. And I was more than happy to return to Amos and the dance floor, with Georgia becoming a forgotten memory.

By the time nine o'clock rolled around, I was almost too tired to stand. The ballroom had a few stragglers still getting their boogie on the dance floor.

My bedtime was approaching, and we still needed to drive home. I walked over to Rosemary to see if she needed anything and saw her struggling with a large crystal punch bowl.

"Rosemary, what are you doing? Don't you have a cleaning crew?" I turned and saw several individuals dressed in black and white folding and stacking tables. Two people were on ladders removing the huge banner off the back wall.

Rosemary responded. "This is my punch bowl. And I wanted to take it to my office, so the crew didn't mistakenly put it with the other dishes."

I leaned in to examine the ornate flowers covering the bowl. "Oh, yeah. I recognize this one. It belonged to your mother."

"Yes, it's one of the few things I have from her. I still have her teapot and all the teacups, too. Can you help me grab the bag? It has some special tablecloths I keep in my office too."

"Sure thing." I reached down to grab the bag, feeling the muscles in my back protest. All that dancing would catch up with me in the morning.

We were headed out of the ballroom when Rosemary stopped, appearing confused.

"What's wrong?" I asked.

"Can you check the bag for my office badge? I can't seem to find my phone either."

I felt around in the bag several times. "Are you sure you put them in here?"

She shook her head. "No, I think I last saw them on the

table where I was sitting. I wonder if someone from the cleanup crew grabbed them. My face is on the badge, so they should have just brought it to me."

"Do you want to go ask them?"

Rosemary sighed. "I'm tired. It will probably be quicker to get the master key from the security guard. My feet are killing me too."

"Okay, I will catch up to you." I spotted Amos and noticed him talking to the DJ, probably admiring his equipment. I didn't know until Amos moved in that he had the largest vinyl music collection I'd ever seen. My youngest child, Leesa, had introduced me to some online music apps like Pandora and Spotify. Amos shunned them, preferring his old school record player. How he kept the ancient equipment in mint condition was a mystery to me.

I waved at him and pointed to Rosemary retreating. "I'm assisting Rosemary with taking some things to her office. I will be ready to go soon."

Amos gave me a head nod.

I hurried to catch up with Rosemary. As we approached the administrative offices, Rosemary stopped, and I stumbled, almost crashing into her.

"What is going on? I thought you were going to get the master key."

She shook her head and pointed. "The door is open. Someone left the doorstop under the door which is against company policy. These doors need to be kept closed for security."

I offered. "Maybe the cleaning crew is still working or needed to return to finish their work. You know folks take breaks."

Rosemary hesitated for a second, her face contorted in

confusion before stepping inside. She shrugged and then pushed the doorstop out of the way with her foot, swinging the door inside.

I'd been in Rosemary's office a few years ago planning my son and my daughter-in-law's wedding reception. The office area had a reception area in the front, and behind the long desk meant to separate visitors from the receptionist were several doors.

Once I stepped inside, my eyes adjusted to the dim light, and then gradually focused on one door that stood wide open. The hairs lifted on my arms. And I started whispering, not even sure why. "Isn't that your office? Did you lock it?"

"I'm pretty sure I did," Rosemary whispered back.

Something wasn't right!

"Should we call someone? I can go get Amos."

"No, let me just get this punch bowl in my office. It's really heavy."

We walked silently behind the receptionist area towards the open door; the carpet muffled our footsteps. When we reached the door, the pitch-black interior appeared ominous, as if someone would jump out. I should have turned around and called Amos, but Rosemary had already stepped closer to the door's threshold. I didn't want to leave my friend defenseless with that enormous punch bowl in her hand, so I tiptoed behind her.

I watched anxiously as Rosemary reached around the wall.

Fluorescent lights lit up the office.

That's when I saw it.

A sequined silver heel. With a foot inside it. My eyes glided up towards the face.

I started screaming. Then I became

conscience of Rosemary matching my hysteria. Her screams and mine were reminiscent of a haunted house tour.

But this wasn't some elaborate horror show setup.

In her fright, Rosemary let her precious punch bowl slip from her fingers. It crashed to the floor, splitting into three large pieces, with one piece gently rocking back and forth near the body.

I slapped my hand over my mouth, but strange moans still leaked through my fingers. This didn't stop my feet from moving further inside the office to examine the victim's face. I had to be sure what I was seeing.

Oh yeah! That's Georgia Hayes.

My eyes stretched at the gash over her right eye.

Rosemary had stopped screaming, but her chest heaved with every breath. She shuffled forward to see where my hands were pointing. She shrieked. "Oh my goodness. Eugeena, is this real?"

I nodded, unable to speak. There was a lot going through my mind at the moment, besides the fact I was looking at yet another dead body. My inquiring mind wanted to know one thing as I turned to face Rosemary.

"What was she doing in your office?"

Chapter 3

Apparently, our screams had attracted attention. Thankfully, most of our classmates had either headed home or to their hotel rooms upstairs.

Amos appeared at the door huffing and puffing like he'd run a 200-meter dash. "What's wrong?"

I stepped to the side so he could see. Now Amos and I had a long conversation about my last adventure. Though he appreciated my willingness to solve a crime, he felt like it was getting to me. Amos, a retired homicide detective, knew seeing dead bodies at various crime scenes eventually would take a toll on one's mental state of mind.

He peered intently at the body. "Eugeena, is that...?"

I nodded. "Yes, that's Georgia Hayes."

Amos rubbed his head. "Okay, both of you get out of this office right now." He pointed to the remains of the sparkling punch bowl. "What's that on the floor?"

Rosemary wailed. "I dropped my mother's punch bowl."

"It broke into large pieces. We might be able to fix it." I tried to soothe Rosemary, which was crazy because I wasn't feeling anything but panic climbing my shoulders.

Oh, Lord, please help us! Poor Georgia, poor, poor woman!

Not to speak ill of the dead, but she was a royal pain in the butt. Still, why would someone kill her? We all had known each other most of our lives. Before and after tonight, most of us would never see each other again unless we're blessed to be alive for the fiftieth high school reunion. These thoughts bombarded my mind as Amos guided us outside of the office.

"This entire office and everything in it is a part of the crime scene. You two are going to be questioned," he said.

Rosemary spun around; her eyes wide. "Questioned? We just found her."

"Yes, and both of you were arguing with her earlier tonight. Everyone saw and someone, if not several people, will mention it to the police."

I huffed. "People know Georgia and they know us. We were both in that ballroom the entire time."

Rosemary looked stricken. "Not the entire time. I had to run in and out to check on the staff."

Amos inquired. "Did you see Georgia?"

Rosemary shook her head. "No, I only saw her when she came up to me in the ballroom."

Amos might have been retired, but the job never left him. "Did you touch her? Did you touch anything else?"

Rosemary waved her hands. "It's my office. My fingerprints are everywhere. Besides that, what was she doing in my office? I don't understand how she got in here."

"Someone took your office badge." I reminded her.

Amos raised his eyebrows at me. He knew what I was doing, but I couldn't help myself on this one. It didn't make a lick of sense, so I continued. "Someone knew to get access to the office they had to get Rosemary's badge."

Rosemary shook her head. "I don't recall Georgia

coming near my table. She wouldn't know anything about this area anyway."

Amos turned to Rosemary. "Before we go accusing Georgia, did you see the badge in there? On the desk? Near the body?"

I shook my head. "I was too busy staring at... Georgia so I didn't notice."

Rosemary gulped. "I don't think I saw it anywhere on the floor or desk. I believe I would have noticed it."

Amos nodded. "Well, it's possible the killer ran off with the badge. Maybe even swiped it from the table."

Questions clogged my mind. "I can't get past what she was doing in Rosemary's office. I thought she'd left and gone home."

Amos warned me. "I agree, it's strange. But we're going to leave this to the police."

"Okay, Amos, I will stay out of this." I turned to Rosemary. "I'm sorry about your Mama's punch bowl."

"Me too. It can't be replaced, but I'm more concerned about bigger things right now. This is a nightmare. Maybe Georgia was right. Maybe I shouldn't have had this reunion at the hotel. The last thing I want to do is bring more bad publicity to the hotel."

"Don't worry about that right now." I knew she was referring to an incident only a year ago when a guest had been found dead in his hotel room. The victim was my current daughter-in-law's first husband.

Oh yeah, and she found him.

That's a whole other story.

I don't know why the Lord had me experience all these horrific events during my retirement years. This amateur sleuth business was not the kind of hobby anyone in their right mind should pick up. But people around me were always getting into trouble.

So much for me trying to avoid it.

In fact, while Amos called the police, I asked Rosemary, "Why do you think Georgia came tonight? She couldn't have just gotten dressed up to pick a fight. Do you think something else riled her up?"

Rosemary narrowed her eyes. "You're right. I reached out to her and all the classmates who hadn't RSVP'd and she refused to come. In fact, she hung up on me."

"So you called her. Kind of like when you called me telling me I shouldn't miss this."

Rosemary chuckled a little. "I was trying to make sure you came. You know I've been so happy for you since you married Amos. I was worried about you when Ralph died and then when you retired."

I frowned. "Worried about me. What about you?" Rosemary had lost her husband to cancer almost ten years ago, but she stayed busy at the hotel and with her family. "Aren't you planning to retire soon?"

She cringed. "I've thought about it, and I know one day my body will not cooperate with me. But I really love what I do here. But now after all this, I don't know, Eugeena. My boss will not be happy about this."

"It's not your fault."

"But you heard what Amos said. People saw us arguing with Georgia. Can you not see how that rumor is going to start and spread? It doesn't matter if I have witnesses or an alibi. I, and maybe even you, will already be judged guilty."

She had a point.

A deputy soon arrived, taking Rosemary to the side for her statement. My friend looked scared, but she had no reason to be. Right? I thought back to earlier. I couldn't help but think that the entire argument seemed petty and just plain silly.

My eyelids grew heavy, and suddenly my thoughts muddled. I blinked to focus my blurry eyes on my watch. It was way past my bedtime now. But I'd never been a party girl.

I glanced up to see a familiar figure approaching. My tired body seemed to sag even more. Sleep might not be an option at all tonight. Of all the detectives at CPD, the Charleston Police Department, Detective Sarah Wilkes had to be the one to show up.

The petite detective looked even more disheveled than usual. Her white blouse, barely tucked into her khaki slacks, wasn't crisp. Detective Wilkes usually wore her long red hair pulled back in a ponytail or a messy bun. Tonight she sported a bob. Her freckles and pointy chin made her seem younger.

Before I could stop by myself, I blurted. "You have a new hairdo, Detective Wilkes."

Wilkes stopped in front of me and gave me a wry smile. "Thank you for noticing. I needed a change. Not the world's best cut, but easy to maintain." The detective looked around. "I hear you all had quite the party. The 1970s, huh?"

Now I cracked a smile. "What do you know about the 70s, Detective? You weren't even born."

"Nope. But you forget this was my dad's era. I believe the man would love it if it was still the 70s."

Detective Wilkes and I had an interesting relationship. It wasn't a friendship but a mutual association. Amos and her dad, Lenny Wilkes, worked together at CPD. Amos still lent a hand in Lenny's private investigation agency.

Detective Wilkes took a moment to look towards the

door where the crime scene techs had entered before turning back to me. "I understand you talked to the victim earlier."

I sighed. "It wasn't much of a discussion, more like trying to figure out why she was so upset and determined to stir up trouble."

"The victim approached you and Mrs. Gladstone?"

"That's correct."

"Did you see where she went after she left the ballroom?"

"I assumed she went home. She didn't want to attend the reunion."

Detective Wilkes whipped out her notebook at that moment. The camaraderie we had a few moments ago was in the past as she took on her official persona. "About what time would you say she left the ballroom?"

I frowned. "I remember "The Hustle" was playing when she left. It's been a while since this old lady got her groove going. Looking at my watch was the least of my concerns."

A slight grin appeared on the detective's face, but it quickly disappeared. She pursed her lips as she jotted notes down in her notebook. "Did you leave the ballroom after she left?"

"No, I didn't."

"Not even to go to the restroom?"

"Oh, yes, I forgot. Rosemary and I went to the ladies' room."

"How long ago was that after the victim left?"

Now I may have been sleepy, but a sharpness woke up my senses. "What are you trying to ask, Detective Wilkes?"

She sighed and then looked up from her notebook.

"Did you have an encounter with the victim outside of the ballroom?"

"If you are asking if I saw her in between when she was acting a fool in the ballroom and then when she was lying dead on the floor of my friend's office, the answer would be no. I thought the woman had gone home."

Detective Wilkes nodded. "Any ideas on why the victim was in Mrs. Gladstone's office?"

"No, but Rosemary couldn't find her office badge. She was going to get the security guard to let her in." I thought for a moment. "Rosemary mentioned her phone was missing too. Did either of those items show up at the crime scene?"

"You know I can't share anything about the crime scene with you, but that's good to know. Now I have another question for you."

"Okay." I wasn't confident that I wanted her to ask me her next question.

"Does your friend, Mrs. Gladstone, have any enemies?"

I started to say other than the one dead in her office but thought better of blurting that. Sometimes I could catch my mouth before something damaging slipped out. That one would have been a doozy.

"Rosemary has always been, and remains, one of the sweetest people I know. She pulled this reunion off with little time, determined to make sure our classmates could come together. We're all getting old and moments like these are pretty special. There's no reason at all for anyone to hate on Rosemary."

"Okay, that's all that I have. If I need anything else, I will get in touch. Have a good night, Ms. Eugeena."

"You too, Detective."

I told Rosemary there was nothing to worry about, but

after that last question, Detective Wilkes had my mind going to other places. I didn't want to scare my friend, but now I wondered if Georgia had been in the wrong place at the wrong time. Instead of being concerned about Rosemary becoming a prime suspect, suppose someone wanted to do my friend harm.

Chapter 4

The next morning, I wasn't sure about going to church, but then I felt a nudge in my spirit. When things were upside down in your life, that wasn't the time to let the spiritual tank get empty. Plus, it was my time to usher and the one thing I didn't want to do was to let down the usher board leaders by not showing up and doing my job. It was only one Sunday a month, and I liked to think I was reliable. So coming across a dead body last night wasn't an excuse.

Amos had other thoughts. "Eugeena, folks will understand. And I'm sure God knows you've been traumatized." He looked at me as if he expected me to fall apart. Then softly added, "Again."

I appreciated my hubby's concerns. I was more upset that Rosemary and I found Georgia. It was sad. But when someone spent their life being mean, their death didn't come as a surprise.

Lord, forgive me.

"I need my church family this morning. I have a feeling Pastor Jones will have a word to share. Georgia wasn't a stranger to Missionary Baptist."

Years ago, Georgia Hayes attended Missionary Baptist

Church. Unlike many people who left over something the pastor said, Georgia clashed with our long-time choir director. Now she had a powerful voice. And she knew it. This meant she enjoyed singing the solo often. All the time if she had the choice. She and the choir director usually bumped heads when it was time for someone else to sing the solo. I don't really know where Georgia attended church after she left. Maybe she sang every Sunday at her new church.

One thing I knew for sure, when I arrived at Missionary Baptist, people knew there had been a murder last night. Even though we were in church, that didn't stop the gossip. Sugar Creek was a small community and our reunion made the eleven o'clock news. If anyone slept through the news last night, the local station had a Sunday morning program that also shared the news. And if folks didn't see the Sunday morning news, Missionary Baptist had our own reporters.

Well, more like queens of the rumor mill. So, while I passed the offering plates from one aisle to the other, I kept getting side glances from my two favorite people. Annie Mae and Willie Mae Brown were special. Their specialness had nothing to do with being twins. They were the nosiest busybodies of the church and knew more information than anybody.

And they had their own history with Georgia. I don't think I'd met anybody who rubbed people the wrong way more than Georgia. The twins at least had their sweet side. When the pastor asked me to run the afterschool and summer programs, I could always count on the Brown sisters to give me a helping hand.

Despite the curious stares from folks in the congregation, Pastor Jones didn't disappoint. In fact, he did what he was great at doing, had me squirming in the back pew as he bellowed, "Love your enemies, church. It's hard to do, but we're called to pray for them instead. That doesn't mean we absolve them from their wrongdoings, but that we are being mindful of our own spiritual walk. When we hold on to things that are not good for us, we become bitter. We become more like our enemy."

I wondered if Pastor Jones had that sermon prepared or if he recalled Georgia's history here. My pastor was a young man back then and his father, Pastor Jones, Sr. had led the church. Anyhow, I needed to hear him preach this morning.

Not too long after service let out, I grabbed my coat from the closet in the usher room only to turn around and find the Brown sisters standing in my way. Annie Mae stood in front with her sister, Willie Mae, peeking over her shoulder. Willie Mae's one good eye had me locked in my place. Her stare was so intense I barely noticed her wandering eye.

I sucked in a breath. "What is it?"

"You know we come to ask you about last night," Annie Mae stated.

I shrugged and began placing an arm inside my coat. "I don't know what happened. Someone killed Georgia."

Willie Mae stepped from behind her sister. "Well, it had to be one of your classmates. Who did it?"

I nodded. "I agree, but I don't know who did it."

"We heard it was Rosemary Gladstone."

Here we go. The rumor mill had started just as Rosemary predicted.

Forgetting my coat, I held my finger up in front of me. "You both know Rosemary. Don't spread that lie in the House of the Lord."

Both twins at least had the sense to look sheepish.

I finished putting my coat on, suddenly feeling too warm. "We need to pray for Georgia's family. Even though she had her issues, no one deserves to be killed like that."

Annie Mae perked up. "How was she killed?"

"Yeah, Eugeena. We know you know the details." Willie Mae added.

Why did people always want to know the details?

"Look, ladies. Amos is waiting for me. And my kids are going to be at the house soon. We're having Sunday dinner. I can't talk about this anymore. All you need to know is it was horrible."

Both sisters stared at me, their eyes wide. Annie Mae commented. "I'm so sorry. You seem upset."

"Yes, I am."

Willie Mae twisted her hands. "We will pray for you, Sister."

"Thank you. I truly appreciate your prayers."

It was football season, and church cleared out pretty quickly. Even Pastor Jones had finished greeting parishioners and appeared to be gone by the time I reached the church's front entrance. As I walked out to the parking lot, it occurred to me I hadn't seen Rosemary during the church service. She always showed up every Sunday unless she was sick. If I was feeling awful about last night, I knew she must have been miserable. We found the woman in Rosemary's office. I couldn't get over our discovery.

Ahead of me, I glimpsed Michelle Gladstone, Rosemary's only child. I called out to her. "Michelle."

The woman turned around. She was the spitting image of her mother; except she had a darker complexion. Standing next to her was her precocious daughter, Amani Gladstone. Amani attended the afterschool program, where she remained until either her mother or her grandmother picked her up.

As I approached, the young girl started bopping up and down. "Hey, Amani. How are you doing?"

"We're doing fine. We gotta get back home. Grandma wasn't feeling well this morning."

Leave it to the children to tell all your business.

I looked at Michelle. I didn't want to alarm Amani, so I asked, "Did your mother tell you about last night?"

Michelle nodded and glanced down at her daughter. "Why don't you open the car?" She gave the little girl her keys. The little girl eyed her mom like she knew something was up, but then ran over to open the car.

Michelle turned toward me. "I'm really worried about mom. When she said you all found that woman in her office, I thought that was the craziest thing I'd ever heard. Why would she be in her office? But then it got me thinking. Do you think someone was after her or were they after my mother?"

That kind of took me aback. It was the same line of questioning Detective Wilkes had asked last night. "But your mother doesn't have any enemies. No one would want to hurt your mother. Right?"

Michelle was quiet for a moment. "You know Mama doesn't like confrontation. She would rather let a situation slide. But since we started living with her, I know someone has been frustrating her at work. She told me the other day she's thinking seriously about retirement. Mama loves her job."

I frowned. "I asked her last night about retirement. She said she knew she had to do it one day."

Michelle nodded. "I have been encouraging her to

consider retirement. But lately, someone at her job has really gotten on her nerves."

"Do you know who?"

"There is one coworker that is related to the hotel CEO. Mom said she is always overstepping her role and trying to get her way. But I don't see anyone wanting to harm my mother. I feel silly for having the thought."

"None of it makes sense, but don't worry. Your mother is going to be fine. Just be there to support her and let me know if you need anything."

I watched as Michelle joined Amani in the car.

Amos had been sitting in the car waiting patiently for me. He was used to me getting sidetracked after church services. As I climbed into the Toyota Camry, I heard the local radio station reporter say, "If you are just tuning in, we want to report the police are still at the Charleston Place Hotel where the second murder in a year took place last night."

"They are still at the hotel?" I inquired.

Amos turned the radio off before responding. "It's a big hotel and the killer had to have left some evidence."

"Well, I hope they find this person quickly. Rumors are flying around thanks to our favorite twins."

Amos chuckled as he guided the car out of the parking lot. "Why am I not surprised? Was that Rosemary's daughter you were talking to?"

"Yes. She's really worried about her mother. I didn't even notice that Rosemary hadn't made it to the church. I'm going to have to call to check on her."

"That's a good idea. Just remember you're going to let Detective Wilkes handle this one."

"No worries! I intend to keep my nose out of it."

But as I said those words, I felt a sharp tingle go down my back, convicting me.

Eugeena, you're not telling the truth.

There was no way I could stay out of this one.

Chapter 5

The kitchen had always been my domain, my comfort zone. I loved cooking but had to admit the older I got and the more I'd tried maintaining my weight loss, being in the kitchen wasn't like it used to be. Usually, we went out to a restaurant after church on Sunday, but the kids had been begging me for Sunday dinner at the house. As much as I cooked when my children were growing up, none of them were interested in learning how to cook.

That was okay. Cooking was good for my soul! After last night's discovery and my growing worries for my friend's safety, I needed to bang around in the kitchen.

Thank goodness I had planned ahead. I figured after attending the reunion that I would be too tired to make Sunday dinner. The slow cooking method had always been a favorite. Minutes later, I stirred the roast beef and vegetables in the slow cooker. The aroma filled the kitchen and lifted my mood.

My aunt Cora gifted us with a rice cooker as a wedding gift. Amos loved his rice and I don't know how I managed without one all these years.

I piled the fragrant jasmine rice on a serving plate. Then poured the roast beef into a large serving bowl. With the food setup, I went to work on the dining room table. My earliest memories as a child involved me setting a table. Today, I had a crowd.

Unfortunately, my oldest Junior and his family were too far away in Greenville, South Carolina. But my youngest son, Cedric, and his wife, Carmen, Leesa, and her boyfriend, Chris, all lived in Charleston. Amos's daughter Briana had moved back home earlier this past spring. She wasn't at church this morning, but I knew she performed last night at Sugar Creek Cafe. She regularly did a few numbers on stage on Saturday evenings. These were all going to be some hungry young people.

Not too long after I had the meal squared away, Leesa and Chris showed up first. I had to smile. These two had been a part of each other's lives for quite a few years, and they had a son together. I learned over the years to not be judgmental. My first marriage was one of those shotgun-kind-of-weddings. I got pregnant my senior year and my father expected Ralph Patterson to take responsibility.

I felt happy that my daughter seemed to be in a good place. There was a time I wasn't too sure about Chris. For several years, Leesa and I didn't get along the way we did now. It paid not to rock the boat and let young people work things out for themselves. We all had to do that in order to grow.

My two grandchildren, Kisha and Tyric, came flying through the kitchen door wide open. Both had their arms wrapped around my legs before I could utter a greeting.

"How are my babies doing today? Did you have a good week?" I often babysat for these two during the week, but Leesa had taken the week off for a change.

"Hey, Grandma." Kisha gushed. "I had a good time in school. I drew a picture of Porgy, but I forgot to bring it."

"That's okay, baby. Bring it the next time you come. What about you, Tyric?"

Tyric answered, "Where's Porgy?"

Okay, so I knew who my grandbabies really came to see. I wasn't offended. Porgy was a rather porky Corgi. I'd inherited the furry package from a friend who had been killed a few years back. I'd never had a pet. Back when my empty nest had been a bit too lonely, that little pup became my companion.

I heard the doorbell rang and then more voices in the living room.

"Mama Eugeena, it smells so good in here."

I looked up to find my daughter-in-law, Carmen standing in the doorway, her hand covering her small baby bump. She and Cedric had been keeping this pregnancy under wraps because of a miscarriage a few months ago. Both parents were obstetricians, so they delivered babies all the time. Carmen expressed some concern a while back about not knowing much about her medical history since she had been adopted. That lack of knowledge, along with the miscarriage, had her down.

I prayed we all could meet this little one next spring. He or she would be grandbaby number six for me.

Cedric had been a bachelor for so long, there was a time I wondered if he would ever get married. He was a superb uncle to his nieces and nephews, and I knew he was going to be a great dad.

"How are you two doing?" I pointed towards Carmen's belly.

"We're doing fine." Carmen rubbed her mound. "The morning sickness seems to have passed."

"I'm glad to hear. You put your feet up and I will serve dinner soon."

Leesa came through the kitchen door, followed by Briana.

Both women hugged Carmen. Leesa exclaimed, "You are glowing! I can't wait to meet the little guy."

Briana asked, "How do you know it's a boy?"

"Just a feeling," Leesa answered. "Mama, the menfolk are already congregating around the television for the football game."

Lord, help me. Football season had always been a struggle for me with a house full of men. While I supported my boys, I never understood the game or the appeal.

After a lot of wrangling, we all were sitting around eating. Amos had the honor of saying grace, which I noticed he'd shortened. I did not know who was playing, but that football game had Amos and the other men scarfing down their food. Everyone seemed to enjoy the beef stew as I observed all the heads bent down towards their plates. This brought me some peace.

That all changed when Leesa piped up and asked, "Mama, what happened at the high school reunion? I saw the news last night. Was that really your classmate?"

I sighed, and my eyes met Amos'. I knew it was too good to be true. We couldn't just have a normal Sunday dinner. My daughter craved drama.

Before I responded, I looked over at the kids' table Amos had built a few months ago. Tyric picked at his food, his hands messy with gravy. Kisha peered wide-eyed at the grown-up table. That child had a curious spirit like her mama. And me.

"Yes, someone..." I cleared my throat, "passed on last night. I hate to admit it, but she was my classmate."

Cedric eyed me; he also looked over his shoulder

towards the kids' table before he spoke. "Why do you hate to admit?"

Amos answered that one for me. "Apparently, your mother didn't get along with the woman. Y'all should know your mama and Rosemary got into it last night with the victim."

Leesa shrieked. "A fight? Not you and Miss Rosemary. I thought you two were dignified."

I dropped my fork, giving up on my meal. "We didn't get into a fight."

"Not physically," Amos commented.

What was wrong with Amos? Why was he making this a big deal?

Cedric had dropped his fork, too. My son loved to eat, though he kept in shape. For him to stop eating, I knew I was in trouble. "So the cops are looking at you?"

"What, of course not?" Then I thought for a minute. I'd had run-ins with Detective Wilkes before. I peered at Amos. "Am I a suspect? Rosemary too?"

Amos shrugged. "You know Detective Wilkes; she will come back with more questions."

"Oh no," Carmen held her belly as if she was protecting her baby. "Ms. Eugeena, you know how she did me last year."

"And me, this past summer," Briana piped up. "That woman is relentless."

I don't know what it was about the people around me and how they attracted attention from law enforcement. We were all good people, minding our own business. Now, here I was in their shoes just because I attended my high school reunion.

Leesa reached over and touched my hand. "Mama, you have to find out who did this."

Cedric slapped the table. "No, she doesn't. Mama has been getting into too much stuff the past few years. Amos, she needs to stay away from this, especially if the police are looking at her."

Before I could open my mouth, Amos stated, "I told her she needs to lie low on this one."

"You told me?" Now, these folks were getting on my nerves.

"I suggested." Amos held up his hands, his face a mask of calmness. "We all know you are going to do what you gonna do."

He was right, and that made me even madder. "Rosemary and I had nothing to do with Georgia Hayes's death. She had no business in Rosemary's office."

The table grew silent after my revelation, all eyes on me.

Leesa sucked in a breath, breaking the silence. "Y'all found her..."

She almost said body but had the good sense to look over at her own children. Both Kisha and Tyric were looking at the adult table, eyes wide.

"You both better finish your food." Leesa admonished. She turned back towards the table, her voice lower. "That wasn't on the news."

"Thank goodness it wasn't or we would have reporters outside the door this morning," Amos commented.

I frowned, my anger deflating like a balloon. "I hadn't thought about that. I wonder why."

"Probably because Detective Wilkes is keeping a tight lid on things." It was the first time Chris could get a word in. He was a large man, but he had a subtle way of blending into the background. He'd been a patrol cop when Leesa first met him. Now a CPD detective, I could see he had a talent for observation, much like Amos, who'd become his mentor.

"That's right. You work with her," I said.

Chris had transferred to the Charleston Police Department as a rookie detective. This brought him closer to Leesa and the children.

Chris nodded. "I haven't worked with her on a case yet, but I've seen her in action. She definitely doesn't like the media. A few weeks ago, Wilkes ranted about leaks and how the media messed up her case. No doubt she has one of the best records at CPD, so it was understandable."

Amos nodded. "She's like a hound dog with a bone. She will definitely be back to question you and Rosemary again. Guaranteed."

Carmen responded. "Well, I can give you the lawyer's name that I had. Thankfully, I never had to use him, but I felt better having him by my side."

I'd met the lawyer that helped Carmen, but I wasn't ready to go there.

Chris added, "I could try to get some intel on the case for you. I don't think Detective Wilkes is aware of my connection to you, Ms. Eugeena."

I shook my head. "No, you're new to the department and you don't need to get on her bad side. Besides, it was a ridiculous disagreement. Everybody heard Georgia whining, and she was notorious for causing a scene, just craving attention. You guys don't need to worry about anything."

I stared at Amos, imploring that he agreed.

He nodded. "No, of course, you all don't have to worry about anything. Besides, your mother promised us she would stay away from the investigation."

"Of course!" I nodded my head dutifully.

We finished the meal with no further discussion. Soon the men were back in the living room yelling at the television as though the coaches and players could hear their playbook rants.

Carmen went upstairs to be with the children while Leesa and I cleared the table.

Briana stopped in the kitchen. "Thanks for the meal, Eugeena. I hate to run but I had a pretty long night."

Amos' daughter and I had a breakthrough this past summer. It made my marriage to her dad that much easier knowing his daughter supported it. "I'm sorry we missed your gig last night."

Briana smiled. "Not a problem. A forty-fifth high school reunion is a once-in-a-lifetime event. Although it sounds like the reunion turned sour towards the end. So sorry all this happened."

"Me too."

After Briana left, Leesa and I stacked dishes in the dishwasher.

Leesa asked, "Mama, you have some ideas about who did this, right? It had to be one of your classmates? If this woman picked a fight with you and Rosemary, she must have made someone else angry enough to kill her."

I looked through the open kitchen door, hoping no one had heard Leesa's questions. I turned to my daughter. "I'm really trying to stay out of this, but yeah, it had to be one of our classmates. Georgia was not well-liked. She was a pretty woman back in the day, but she always had a horrible attitude. She would say things to people behind their back and to their face."

"Sounds like a mean girl," Leesa stated matter-of-factly. "Did she like to bully people?"

I nodded, "Probably. The girls she hung around with

seemed to fear her. Now she was really jealous of Rosemary. She considered her competition. My goodness, I even got into it with her in high school."

"You? I thought you were one of the quiet, studious girls?" Leesa snickered.

Yeah, people liked to joke about the quiet ones. Sometimes what they said was true, other times people just made stuff up about what they didn't know. I stayed quiet; I knew my smart mouth would get me in trouble. I had enough sense back then, but the older I'd become... I had to pray for forgiveness over the things I said.

I took a breath, realizing I was about to share something with my daughter that the past me wouldn't have shared. Our relationship had truly changed. "She dated your father."

"What?" Leesa almost dropped the dish she was attempting to fit on the dishwasher rack. "She dated Daddy."

I grabbed a towel to wipe down the counter. "They broke up and your dad started following me from class to class. I couldn't believe it at first. She really had a hard time seeing him pursue me. I was not in her league, especially in the looks department. She was furious when we started dating. Every chance she had, she had something to say. When I got pregnant with Junior, that girl was relentless."

"Wow, that's crazy. She was a hot mess! What did Daddy see in her?"

I shook my head. "You know I asked him that one time. He said he thought she was pretty, but then every time she opened her mouth, he saw her differently. Her mean ways morphed her into something else."

"Mmmm, that's what having an ugly attitude will do for you." Leesa closed the dishwasher and pushed the start button. She sidled over to me, and with a low voice said, "You don't have to tell the others, but I know you are going to look for who did this. I know you, Mama."

I couldn't even respond; my daughter was not telling a lie. One of my classmates killed Georgia Hayes. I wasn't about to let Rosemary or myself take the blame.

Chapter 6

Monday morning, I laid in bed longer than usual. Amos and our furry shadow, Porgy, had their own morning routine. Both males enjoyed bonding time outside in the backyard. Sometimes they walked around the neighborhood. I took advantage of my alone time to remain in bed. Funny how a few years ago, I struggled with being alone. My family of five had been my life until they all left one by one. As a retired schoolteacher, I had to learn to give my body permission to rest. All those mornings of getting up at 5 a.m. and then doing morning duty at the school bus lane were far behind me.

Unfortunately, this morning, my body felt like I had dragged it while I slept. Probably because I woke up every hour with Leesa's words on my mind. I fibbed at the dinner table yesterday to appease everyone, but I had to know who killed Georgia. My thoughts bombarded me so much I hadn't noticed Amos' return.

"Eugeena, are you okay? You're in bed later than usual this morning. I know you are not sleeping."

I peeked out from under the covers at him. "How do you know?"

"For one, I didn't hear you snoring."

I rolled my eyes and flipped the cover off my body. "I told you I don't snore."

"I'm just joking." His smile faded. "But you were tossing and turning all night. Were you having a nightmare? Do you want to talk to someone about what happened a few months ago?"

I shook my head. "Believe it or not, I'm no longer beating myself up about not seeing the culprit before it was too late."

He sat on the bed next to me. "So is it Georgia Hayes? It couldn't be easy finding her body. I've been wondering if Saturday night triggered other events you've witnessed."

I stood and stretched. "Nope." I should just spit out what's on my mind, but I felt the need to stall. "Let me get a shower and then I will start some breakfast. You mind starting the coffee."

He nodded. "I prepped the coffee pot while Porgy was outside. The coffee should start brewing in a few minutes."

"Good, I will be down in the kitchen shortly."

The shower helped knock away some cobwebs. As I shuffled down the stairs, I could smell turkey bacon. Amos had been a widow for several years, so I was pretty impressed that he didn't mind doing his part in the kitchen. I arrived in the kitchen; Amos sat at the table, and Porgy gave me the eye as he munched on his kibbles. "Good morning to you, Porgy."

The dog grunted in between his crunches. I grabbed my meter from the counter and checked my glucose levels. After my doctor had diagnosed me with Diabetes II two years ago, I'd been determined to take the weight off so I wouldn't have to inject insulin. Between exercise and eating better, I'd been able to keep my glucose, or as my grandmother called it, sugar, on track. My levels were usually a little low in the morning, which could explain why I stayed in bed much longer, too.

By the time we had eaten part of our breakfast, I'd felt a bit more confident about what I had to say. "There is something I should talk about with you."

Without looking at me, Amos stated, "You aren't going to sit this one out, are you?"

Surprised, I looked up with my mouth still full. I chewed and swallowed quickly. "How did you know? Did you overhear Leesa talking in the kitchen yesterday?"

He raised an eyebrow. "No, I didn't. I just know you. I know you can't let this go, especially since you and Rosemary are involved. Plus, you've been too quiet, which means the wheels are turning in that head of yours."

I sighed. "I really feel bad about not telling the truth, but I didn't want the children to be concerned. And I don't want to let you down either. I know you've been worried."

"I just don't want you to bite off more than you can chew. So, do you have any ideas about who did this?"

I shook my head. "Not a clue. I'm assuming it's one of my classmates. Although Michelle said something that troubled me. She wondered if maybe the killer was after her mother. Detective Wilkes hinted at it, too. But Rosemary and Georgia have such different body types. Even if it was dark, would someone mix them up?"

Amos rubbed his head. "It's possible. I'm sorry, but this could be about Rosemary. I thought about bringing it up with you but didn't want to upset you. But it looks like this has been on your mind. What does Rosemary say?"

"I haven't talked to her about it. Her daughter said her mother was having issues with a co-worker."

Amos commented. "Rosemary doesn't seem like the kind to have enemies."

"She's not. Well, I guess technically Georgia was an enemy of hers, but that was ancient history. It really upset her about Georgia not appreciating all her efforts to host the reunion."

Amos pushed his empty plate away and crossed his arms. "It looked like two enemies facing off on Saturday."

"Yeah, and I was right in the middle." I began clearing the dishes off the table. "Nothing explains why Georgia was in Rosemary's office. Someone swiped Rosemary's key and phone. Any ideas?"

"Would Rosemary have something in her office that Georgia wanted?"

"I doubt it." I frowned. "But then again, I don't know. Rosemary was bringing her mother's punch bowl back to her office. She obviously felt like her office was a safe place for something that sentimental."

"These were the administrative offices. Perhaps there's a safe or something that presents value."

I sat down as I mulled over Amos' theories. "There was an incident back in high school where someone was stealing things out of people's lockers. Rosemary had a bracelet go missing. Someone claimed that Georgia had been hanging around. But that was never proven and honestly, I don't see why Georgia would hang around to commit a robbery. She seemed bent on leaving the reunion and she should have been home."

"Something or someone must have convinced her to stay," Amos commented.

That's when the fog in my brain cleared. "Wait, her ex-husband went after her. He said he was going to talk to her."

"The guy with the enormous arms. I've seen him before."

"He's Jimmy Hayes, the owner of the Chicken Shack. Remember, they catered for the reunion. Anyway, Jimmy's father started the business when he was in middle school. Jimmy took over the business after his father grew ill and has expanded it to four restaurants in the Lowcountry. Two restaurants are here in Charleston, one in North Charleston and the other, the very first one, here in the Sugar Creek community."

"I see. You said they're divorced. I wonder if Georgia still receives alimony from him."

My eyes grew wide. "She certainly could. I heard they divorced a few years back. They would have been together for a long time. Are you trying to say Jimmy might have gotten rid of her so he didn't have to pay her money anymore?"

"Slow down, Eugeena. It's a possibility. Do you know if they have children?"

I frowned, "I know she had a son not too long after I had Junior, but I honestly stopped keeping up with Georgia, especially after she left Missionary Baptist."

Amos raised his eyebrows. "So you all attended the same church?"

"Yes. I will say Georgia wasn't the world's nicest person, but she had a beautiful voice and brought a lot to the choir." I sighed. "She had a lot of things going for her, but she seemed bent on being destructive. I don't know what made her the way she was. As long as I have known her, I actually know little about her."

"That could be the key to finding her killer. Her disagreement with you and Rosemary may have just been her blowing off steam. She couldn't do anything about another situation."

I nodded. "It was strange. I got the sense she really

missed her friend Pauline. Maybe if she had stepped forward and took over for her, maybe planning the reunion would have made her happy."

I didn't have time to dwell on it. My phone was ringing. I looked around for it. "Do you know where I left my phone?"

"Sounds like the ringing is coming from upstairs."

I heaved myself up from the kitchen table to make my way back up the stairs.

This better not be one of those robocalls.

I headed towards the stairs, this time with Porgy at my feet. I wasn't sure why he suddenly had the energy to run past me upstairs. When I reached the bedroom door, Porgy ran circles around the bedroom. I think the dog liked my new ringtone.

The phone had stopped ringing, but when I glanced down at the caller ID, I saw Rosemary had called and left a voicemail. Now that alarmed me. I pressed play on the voicemail. "Eugeena, I have had the most awful morning and wished I hadn't even come to work today. I had the worst confrontation with my boss. I may lose my job after all the years." Rosemary's wail at the end of the call had me in tears. "Eugeena, I'm not a murderer."

Oh, dear Lord, why is this happening to my friend?

I called Rosemary back several times before she picked up the phone. "Rosemary, are you okay? Where are you?"

"I'm home. No, I'm not okay."

"They fired you?"

"Not yet, but it certainly felt like I had been dismissed. Eugeena, what am I going to do? This just makes me look even more guilty? I've worked for the Charleston Place Hotel for twenty-five years, and I get treated like this for something that was completely out of my control."

"We're going to find out who did this." As I stated this out loud, my mind tried to think about next steps. "You sent invites to all the classmates, right?"

"Yes, that's correct. I have a list. Why?"

"I think we need to reach out to our classmates."

"Eugeena, is that really a good idea? Don't you think the detective will do that? I believe she has a copy of the reunion attendees."

"I have no doubt that Detective Wilkes will do her job, but isn't it bothering you we missed something last Saturday night? Besides, you don't need to be alone right now. Let's look through the list and maybe we can give Detective Wilkes some better ideas."

"That sounds like a plan. I will be over in about thirty minutes."

When I got off the phone, I turned to see Amos standing in the doorway of our bedroom. "What?"

"What was that about?" he asked.

"Rosemary is on the verge of losing her job, Amos. Who knows what Detective Wilkes is thinking; we have to do something."

Amos sat down on the bed next to me. "I need to keep you out of trouble. So, what's your plan?"

I leaned over and kissed Amos on the cheek. "I love and appreciate you. Rosemary will be over shortly. I asked her to bring the list of classmates who attended the reunion. She said Detective Wilkes has the same list, so we will look at the same information, except we have an advantage."

He raised an eyebrow. "How so?"

"These are our classmates. We've known each other most of our lives. Who do you think they will talk to more willingly? Us or Detective Wilkes?"

Amos eyed me. "You may have a point, but one of those classmates could be a killer too."

That was sobering.

"Well, I guess you will need to have my back again."

Chapter 7

Rosemary arrived at the front door about an hour after she called. When I opened the door, I could tell she'd been crying. Her eyes were red-rimmed, but she was smiling. That was my friend, always trying to have the glass half full mindset.

"Come in. You made it over here in record time."

Rosemary entered. "I'm so stunned by what happened this morning. I really need a friend right now; I don't know what's going on."

I guided her into the kitchen where Amos remained.

"Hey, Amos." Rosemary pulled out a chair from the table. "I was just telling Eugeena I do not know what is going on."

"Well, we will do our best to help you sort this out."

"I made a fresh pot of coffee, Rosemary. Would you like some?"

"Yes, Eugeena. That would be wonderful."

I set three steaming mugs of black coffee on the table with a bowl of sugar cubes, Splenda packets, and a small pitcher of cream in the middle of the table. Then I sat down next to Amos, so we could both face Rosemary.

Amos asked her. "Tell us what happened at work today."

Rosemary dropped two sugar cubes in her coffee. "When I arrived at work today, the police had my office taped off. My co-workers were ecstatic to see me; everyone thought something had happened to me. That was weird enough, but then no one was allowed in their offices either. After the detective interviewed everyone, folks were looking at me like it was all my fault."

"I'm so sorry." I offered.

"Detective Wilkes really didn't help matters, especially when Mr. Montague, the owner of the hotel showed up. He doesn't show his face often, but Charleston Place was his first hotel. His pride and joy. The man is in his late seventies and owns quite a few hotels, so he's always traveling. But he was born and raised in Charleston, and his primary home is here, so I guess he was in town." Rosemary sipped her coffee before continuing. "Mr. Montague ranted so much I thought he would have a heart attack."

"Oh my," I stated. "The hotel does have a stellar reputation."

"Yes. To be honest, the hotel took a hit last year with the murder at the hotel."

Amos frowned. "The keynote speaker, Darius Randall?"

Rosemary nodded. "Yes, Mr. Montague didn't like how I handled the publicity, which was silly because all I do is book the events and conferences. I'm not the public relations officer. How would anyone have known that a celebrity would be killed in his hotel room?"

I added, "And you certainly wouldn't have known what

was going to happen Saturday night. Georgia didn't show interest in attending the reunion."

Rosemary held her hand to her face as if ashamed. "When I told him someone stole my access badge, it made me appear like an irresponsible employee who doesn't care about the security of our guests and employees. Those were his words."

Amos asked. "I wonder if your office badge and phone have shown up yet."

Rosemary shook her head. "I asked Detective Wilkes about it. She told me neither had been found at the crime scene. So whoever did this still has both. The only good thing, no one can use the access badge again."

I looked at Amos. "They probably can't use her phone either, right? Not without alerting where the phone is located."

Amos nodded. "That's true. I'm puzzled by the missing phone, though. I wonder how it was used or maybe they took the phone to keep the attention off the badge."

"That's a good question. So Rosemary, did they give you a new key?" I asked.

"That's the thing, Eugeena. No, they didn't. Mr. Montague told me I should go home. I asked him for how long, and he said he would be in touch. They could use this to push me out before I'm even ready to retire."

"That's awful, Rosemary. You don't deserve any of this." I hadn't brought this up yet with Rosemary, but now seemed like a good time. "Rosemary, I talked to Michelle on Sunday after service. She mentioned you were having issues with a certain co-worker?"

Rosemary sighed. "I probably shouldn't vent to Michelle, but there is one person who suddenly seems interested in learning what I've been doing the past twenty-five years."

I leaned closer. "Does this person seem like a vindictive person?"

Rosemary's eyes grew wide. "No, I wouldn't say that. She's a bit of a narcissist. And it doesn't help that she's the owner's niece."

I raised an eyebrow. "Oh really. Sounds like a bit of entitlement there."

"Eugeena, that describes Catalina Montague perfectly. Now that I think about it, I wouldn't put it past her to make a stink about all of this, giving her uncle no choice but to come to the hotel. I tell you it really surprised me to see him. I knew it wasn't good."

"I can imagine, but folks will do some underhanded things to get what they want. Still, she sees you every day. You and Georgia have two different body types. It's not like someone could have mistaken you."

Rosemary shuddered. "Are you asking if Catalina mistakenly thought Georgia was me? Oh, Eugeena, I can't let my mind go there. You know me. I don't like trouble. The Lord says to be good to our enemies and while that's hard to do, I have always practiced that principle. I can't imagine somebody would want to kill me."

Amos interrupted. "Rosemary, don't worry. We just want to cover all the bases. I believe we should keep an eye on this Catalina. She does feel suspicious, but there are other factors."

I eyed Amos. "Like we have no idea why Georgia was in your office."

Amos crossed his arm. "Yeah. Rosemary, I believe you brought the list of classmates. The most obvious motive has to be from someone who knew Georgia."

Rosemary bit her lip while blinking rapidly. "I have the list, but maybe we should leave this to the police. Eugeena, I'm scared now. Someone we know probably did this."

I nodded. "It's scary, but I kind of want to know. It's not like we run into our classmates all the time, but if I'm in the grocery store and see someone, I don't want to wonder."

"Why would someone our age do this? There is too much to do with the rest of our lives."

I'd been wondering the same thing.

"Maybe they just snapped. Let's see the list."

We looked at the printout that Rosemary brought with her. I had to admit the listing brought unexpected feelings for me. There were only forty-one out of a class of fifty-four students still alive. And even though she had the worst demeanor, someone still had the nerve to take out one of our classmates.

I took the list and began jotting names in my notebook. I kept a lot of notebooks hanging around the house from my days as a teacher and often used them to record ideas. This one had become my suspect notebook. Seriously, I should be able to write my true crime memoir one day. After I jotted down a few names, I added asterisks beside three for starters.

Rosemary looked at me with awe. "You have turned into a detective, Sistah."

"I don't know about all that, but she certainly tries." Amos winked at me.

I couldn't believe I blushed.

Amos pointed toward the notebook. "Why those people?"

I explained. "Jimmy Hayes is the ex-husband. I want to know what Jimmy said to Georgia when she left."

Amos looked at me. "Are you sure you should talk to him? Suppose he's the killer?"

Rosemary waved her hand. "Jimmy wouldn't hurt a fly. He and my husband were cousins."

"I didn't know that. Now that I think about it, there is some resemblance to your husband."

"They were like brothers."

In the past decade since his death, Rosemary rarely talked about her husband, Lawrence Gladstone, and she never showed interest in remarrying. She smiled. "I agree. Jimmy would be easier to talk to."

Amos sighed. "I don't know. I really don't think either of you should put yourself in danger."

"We won't, Amos. Rosemary and I can meet with him in a public place. The one thing I have learned is to stay away from private properties, like people's homes."

Amos rubbed his head as if he was still unsure. "I guess the public place strategy should work. Rosemary, are you sure you can go along?"

She nodded. "I think I want to know what Jimmy has to say, too. Besides, it's not like they want me back at work."

I pointed to the list. "Rosemary and I also had a conversation with these two ladies. I think it's important that we approach them."

Rosemary peered at where I pointed. "Oh, yeah, Claudia and Sharise joined us in the restroom." She frowned and looked at me. "I remember Sharise sounded really bitter. Did you get the same impression?"

"Yes, Sharise was like a powder keg."

Rosemary stared off. "Georgia used to tease Sharise something awful. She'd always been the shortest person in our class."

"That's right! What about Claudia? Wasn't she bullied by Georgia too?"

Rosemary shrugged. "I think they got along, but Claudia was the timid type. Definitely a follower."

"Yeah, Georgia had her select people who she picked apart, including you."

Rosemary added. "Sometimes you too."

Appeasing Amos, I stated. "So we will follow the same rules. For Jimmy, we can meet him at the Chicken Shack. The ladies, let's invite them to Sugar Creek Cafe, but separately."

Amos grinned. "If you go to the Chicken Shack, be sure to bring back some chicken."

I chuckled. "I pegged you as a fried chicken man and you have not proven me wrong."

Rosemary laughed. "You two are a trip! Now we're going to have to call Jimmy and hope he's available in the Charleston restaurant. He travels between Charleston, Mount Pleasant, and Beaufort. And I heard he's starting up a new restaurant in Savannah."

"Really now. He's quite the business owner. Who'd guessed that when we were in high school?"

"I know. I teased him the other day about not being the smartest person. He used to like to copy my math papers."

Amos picked up the list. "Speaking of math, do you want me and my crew to tackle the rest of this list? You ladies will wear yourself out trying to get in touch with everyone."

"That would be great, Amos."

I appreciated him supporting me even though he had misgivings about my involvement. If I was being honest, I had my own concerns. But I couldn't let this go. In the back of my mind, I really wanted to know what happened after Georgia left the ballroom. So many people could have killed the woman years ago.

Figures the one high school reunion I attend, there was a murder to solve.

Chapter 8

The smell of fried chicken wafted into my nostrils as Rosemary and I entered the Chicken Shack. While the restaurant may have shack in the title, it had a fine dining vibe. The atmosphere felt like you were inside someone's dining room but with lots of dinner guests.

There were booths and tables built with rich mahogany wood, and the chairs had burgundy leather cushions. Menu items were served on real dishes with silver utensils, while Tina Turner belted out "What's Love Got to Do With It" in the background. I never heard music beyond the eighties whenever I visited the Chicken Shack.

Rosemary and I sat at a table in the back. I'd called Jimmy this morning and told him we wanted to stop by to talk. I made the conversation seem as if we wanted to support him during this tough time, which was true. But we also had our questions.

I had given up deep-fried chicken years ago to keep my weight and diabetes at bay, but occasionally, I had an oven-baked recipe I used. While Jimmy served southern fried chicken, he also appealed to vegans and had a form of fried chicken made with tofu. For the more weight-conscious folks like me, the menu offered oven baked rotisserie.

After we gave our lunch orders to the young server, I asked her. "Can you let Jimmy know his classmates are here? We'd love to talk to him and see how he's doing."

"Yes, ma'am," the server smiled.

My eyes wandered to a photo on the wall above us that included Jimmy and his dad. Jimmy was young, but he towered over his dad. He must have gotten his height from his mother's side of the family.

I pointed to the framed portrait. "It's a shame Jimmy looks so intimidating; he's really a big teddy bear. I know Amos has his suspicions, but I can't see it."

"Me neither," Rosemary frowned and then whispered. "Here he comes. Just a warning, he looks awful."

Jimmy had always been a handsome man. Now, with his silver-laced groomed beard and mustache, he was what the ladies called a silver fox and he still had a full head of hair. Locally famous for his family restaurant, Jimmy had also staked out a high school career as a linebacker. He later played for South Carolina State University, his dad's alma mater.

His eyes were red-rimmed and he walked more stooped over than I recalled from the reunion.

As he approached, I said, "I'm really sorry about Georgia."

Jimmy sat down heavy in the chair. "I can't believe she's gone. But I have to say, I'm not surprised."

"You're not?"

"Y'all know how Georgia was. She's always been ornery. The crazy thing, she's just been a hurt little girl all these years. And she made things worse with her mouth."

I had to ask. "What happened on Saturday when she left? Were you asking her to stay?"

Jimmy shook his head. "No, I told her to go home. I saw her walk out the door to the parking lot myself."

"Really?" I raised an eyebrow.

"Yes. She was hopping mad, pacing back and forth outside the ballroom. I told her she did enough damage, and that this was not what Pauline would have wanted."

I thought about her statement. "She must have really missed her best friend."

Jimmy commented. "Her only friend, well, besides me."

"You were too good for her." Rosemary commented.

"She was in her frame of mind that no amount of talking would help. Unfortunately, she always had issues with people she thought were putting her down."

I protested. "Putting her down. She tossed out insults when no one even did anything to her."

"That's right." Rosemary agreed. "She plain didn't like the air I breathed."

Jimmy nodded. "She definitely had her insecurities."

I shook my head. "I always wondered why. She... was a pretty woman, but her attitude was poor."

Jimmy bent his head as if in deep thought. "I don't want to get too much into her business because she was private. But she had a bad upbringing. Let's just say the women in Georgia's house were not beauty queens. Georgia's dad was a very handsome man, but he definitely used and abused Georgia's mother. So she grew up looking different and feeling the wrath of a bitter woman. It took me a long time to learn, but she had nowhere to go with that frustration than on other people."

Rosemary and I stayed quiet for a moment over this revelation.

I finally responded. "It's a shame. Family is where you feel support. Even though I had my first child before I graduated high school, my family was there for me. Not to say they weren't disappointed."

Rosemary nodded. "Yeah, I grew up without my father, but my mother and her sisters were a tight bunch. They encouraged me all the time."

Jimmy looked up at the portraits on the wall. "I experienced good times growing up. My dad could be a hard man sometimes, but he had a good sense of humor. Running a business came naturally for him."

I grinned. "You inherited his business sense. I hear you are opening another Chicken Shack."

Despite the weariness on his face, a smile broke through. Jimmy always had the prettiest white teeth. They were yellowing with age now, but his smile seemed just as bright. "We are opening up number five in Savannah in two weeks."

"You are big time now." I exclaimed. "I'm so proud of you."

Jimmy smiled even wider. While I couldn't tell, I was pretty sure he was blushing.

Then he said, "Georgia said that to me a few weeks ago. Getting a positive comment out of that woman was like pulling a new toy from a baby."

"Sounds like she had her moments," I said.

Jimmy sighed. "She did. At the time we were at our son's grave."

That alarmed me. I remembered their son when he was a little boy. After Georgia left Missionary Baptist, I'd lost track of him.

Rosemary and I exchanged glances. We all had our own lives raising kids and later spoiling our grandkids. I heard bits and pieces about my classmates over the years, mainly through the grapevine. Somehow, I'd missed this. I inquired, "When did Jason die?"

Jimmy closed his eyes. "Almost a year ago. He left home soon as he turned eighteen. Barely graduated. He always had issues in school. Folks bullying him. He took more after Georgia's family, a tall slim fellow. Basketball wasn't his thing, though. Georgia stayed on him, called him lazy even before he turned twelve. She had a way of nagging that could drive a person into the ground."

Rosemary reached over and touched Jimmy's hand. "What happened? I'm so sorry. After Lawrence died, I'm afraid I haven't kept up with your family like I used to. If I'd known..."

Pain flashed across Jimmy's face. "I'm not surprised you didn't know. We kept quiet about Jason's troubles. You know how people talk. He fell in with the wrong crowd. Got on drugs. Every time we tried to get him clean, he went right back. He lived with me, and then he lived with Georgia. He stole from both of us."

Jimmy fell silent. The murmurs of the other restaurant patrons filled in the quiet at our table. I took a moment to take a swig of my tea. My throat felt parched, and I ended up gulping down more. This visit with Jimmy had turned out to be more revealing than I thought. Not in the way I hoped, but sometimes the Lord slid open a door that He wanted you to take a peek inside. You could never really understand a person unless you walked in their shoes. My empathy for Georgia had unexpectantly risen.

Jimmy snatched a napkin out of the silver dispenser on the table and wiped his eyes. "They say Jason overdosed. It was surprising because he was doing so well. Clean for almost two years. Georgia found him. That was the worst day of my life. Poor Georgia couldn't handle it. First time I really saw her fall apart. She hadn't been right since then, not leaving the house much. I had to plan Jason's funeral. In fact, I'm working on Georgia's final arrangements. Crazy, but when we were standing at our son's grave, she asked me to make sure I lay her to rest beside her boy. She loved him so much but she didn't know how to show him."

Something in me broke. I looked over at Rosemary whose face had grown red, tears in her eyes too.

I thought about my children and how heartbroken I would be if one of them left this Earth before me. "I'm so sorry, Jimmy."

Rosemary reached for a tissue and wiped her eyes. "I'm sorry too. I did not know. I always had a feeling Georgia was a hurt person dishing out the hurt. My mother always taught me it's not always the person, but all the stuff that's eating them up inside. Sounds like poor Georgia had her share."

Georgia's words came back to me at that moment.

Maybe I should be grateful that nothing has changed. Everything else has.

"She really had lost a lot. No wonder she was griping at Rosemary about the reunion. Makes the way she died even more tragic." I added. "Jimmy, you know we found Georgia in Rosemary's office. The cops nor Rosemary's boss are looking kindly at her right now. Why would Georgia come back after leaving? Are you sure she left?"

He frowned. "I'm pretty sure she walked out. She was in a huff. In fact, she was moving so fast she almost ran into the valet guy. Poor guy had to scramble out of her way to get back to his booth."

I asked, "Have the cops talked to you yet?"

He nodded. "Oh, yeah, a few times. A little short detective. Believe me, she has her eye on me too, ladies."

"I know Detective Wilkes; she is thorough and worrisome." I crossed my arms, looking around the restaurant. It had grown late in the afternoon and the lunch crowd had left. "Did you notice if any of the other classmates talked to Georgia before or after she left?"

Jimmy shook his head. "No, I don't remember anyone else talking to her. I didn't even know she was at the reunion until I saw her arguing with you two. If she had stayed home like she intended, I wouldn't be planning her funeral."

I had questions about that too. "Georgia doesn't have any other family to do that?"

He grimaced. "Georgia's family started dying out when Jason was young. We stayed separated on and off for years. We often got back together, mainly to support Jason's recovery from his recurring drug habit. Sometimes she didn't help with her tough love. She loved him but she was so hard on him."

"I still don't understand how all this fell on you. She had a church family, didn't she?"

He looked away from us for a few seconds as if trying to find a way to explain. "Georgia stopped going to church years ago when she had the falling out at Missionary Baptist. She claimed all she wanted to do was sing and the choir director didn't like her. It turned her off."

My eyes grew wide. "Okay, there are two sides to that coin for sure."

Jimmy smiled. "I know. Georgia was a complicated and often very opinionated woman. She always was on the unpopular side."

"Jimmy, the delivery guy is here."

We all turned around. A woman had walked up to the table so quietly that none of us had noticed. The woman wore an apron, her dark complexion shining. She was stunning despite having been in the kitchen. Her hair was pulled back and covered with a hairnet. She blinked, showing off lashes that were naturally long.

Jimmy smiled. "I will be there in a second. Florida, these are my classmates, Eugeena Patterson and Rosemary Gladstone. Y'all, this is my wife. We will celebrate our third anniversary in two weeks."

For a moment I forgot to speak. I hadn't realized Jimmy had gotten remarried too. I commented, "Nice to meet you, Florida. This truly is a family business with everyone working."

Jimmy nodded. "Yes, Florida has been with the Chicken Shack for five years. One of my best hires. I had no idea this good-looking woman was going to be my wife one day."

The woman gave a toothy grin, her eyelashes fluttering. "Oh, stop, Jimmy. I appreciate him hiring me back then. I was one broke thirty-five-year-old. Laid off from my job, but I'd always loved cooking."

Jimmy stood and beamed down at his wife. "Sizzled your way into my heart, sweet thing."

I studied Florida a bit more, calculating the difference in age in my head. Jimmy got him a young wife the second time around. There were twenty-two years between them. Well, he had the sugar daddy looks and means to pull it off.

Rosemary asked. "Don't you work on the catering side? I feel like we've met before. Charleston Place Hotel has a contract with the Chicken Shack to cater certain events when clients request catering."

"Yes, I've met with you a few times. Good to see you and thank y'all for letting us cater the reunion. It was so much fun. I'm a product of the nineties but that seventies music was jamming." Florida did a little wiggle.

Jimmy grinned like he'd won a prize. He placed his arm around his wife. "Florida is one of the managers for this restaurant, which y'all know is the original one and serves as headquarters. The catering side is definitely her baby and something she brought to the table when she came."

I loved how Jimmy beamed over his wife's accomplishments.

"Thank you, babe. Ain't nothing like a man bragging about his woman." She winked.

Rosemary and I both chuckled. It was good to see Jimmy happy, especially since he had been weighed down by his ex-wife and losing his son.

From the corner of my eye, I saw a young man step into the restaurant from the back. "Hey, Mr. Hayes, I need your signature."

Jimmy gave the man a head nod, his face somber again. "I appreciate you all stopping by. Not many other people are going to show concern. If you want to stop by, Georgia's funeral will be at 1 p.m. on Friday. Pastor Jones extended Missionary Baptist church to us since Georgia was still on the membership roll. Now, I've made our delivery guy wait too long. Y'all ladies have a good evening."

As Jimmy headed towards the back, Florida reached for our empty plates on the table. "Thank you for looking in on Jimmy. He's such a good man."

I had to ask since she was the new wife. "I guess you knew Georgia well, too."

Florida paused and then grimaced. "Unfortunately, yes.

She and I didn't see eye to eye. She really resented when Jimmy married me."

I said, "I'm glad Jimmy remarried. I recently went down the aisle for a second time myself."

"Congratulations," Florida beamed for a minute before the smile left her face. "It was perfect timing. We were married a few years before his son passed. He was a good man too. Just a bit lost. His mama didn't help him either."

"Well, parents do the best they can. From what Jimmy told us, Georgia didn't have the best role models either."

Florida spoke quietly. "Yeah, I hope she's at peace now."

"Amen to that," I said, and I meant it.

"Can I get you all anything to take home with you?" Florida asked.

"Yes, I'd like to order a bucket of chicken for dinner tonight."

Rosemary smiled. "That sounds like a good idea. Michelle and Amani would love some chicken for dinner too."

"Well, alright now. Let me get someone from the back to get right on your order."

In the next fifteen minutes, they provided both Rosemary and I large plastic bags full of good smelling food. I ordered a bucket of half fried chicken for Amos and half rotisserie chicken for myself. The macaroni and cheese tasted almost as good as mine. That with a side of green beans and honey-flavored biscuits should make my Amos a happy man.

Florida waved at us as we left. "Y'all ladies have a good day."

While Rosemary and I walked towards our cars, she asked. "So what did you think?"

"I think Jimmy likes his women representing the states. Georgia. Now, Florida."

Rosemary burst out laughing, "Oh, Eugeena."

I laughed. "Okay, on a serious note. I don't think Jimmy had anything to do with Georgia's death. Our conversation confirmed to me he's a good man who still cared for a person who didn't deserve him. I am curious about one thing though."

Rosemary asked, "What's that?"

"I know you aren't really at work now, but if I remember correctly with the incident last year, there are cameras at the hotel, especially in the lobby."

Rosemary brightened and snapped her fingers. "Yes, there are. And I can get someone to look at the video."

"Are you sure? It may be easier for Amos or one of his buddies to get that footage. You don't want to get yourself further into hot water."

"That's true, but let Amos know I can connect him with the right person. Why do you want to see the footage? I thought you believed Jimmy."

"Oh, I believe what he said that she left. I'm more interested in when and why she returned. Something or more like someone led her to your office."

To me, that was the burning question that could lead to the murderer.

Chapter 9

Amos munched on the fried chicken as if I hadn't been feeding him. In between licking his fingers, he said, "Man, this is some good chicken. Not as good as yours, of course."

I laughed. "This is a treat. I can't make chicken like this anymore."

Amos swallowed. "You know, we used to stop by the Chicken Shack all the time for lunch. It's a favorite with the force. I'd seen Jimmy before but didn't know he was your classmate until we went to your reunion."

"Small world here in Charleston. You know, after talking to Jimmy today, I kind of feel bad about Georgia. I mean, of course, I hated she was killed, but I don't have any good memories of her, especially the last few hours before her death. But the people close to us always do the most damage."

Amos placed the chicken bone down on the plate with a clatter. "My dad was a hard man to please. I can't say he ever said he loved me or recall if he ever gave me a hug. But I know he did the best he could do. At some point, we all become responsible for how we treat others. And as old as we all are, we should know better."

I sat back and crossed my arms. "You would think, but if being good to other people is something you never put into practice, you only get worse with age."

"So, is that all you found out today? A little history about Georgia."

"Unfortunately, yeah. I hope you fared better than Rosemary and I did with our interview today. Speaking of progress, weren't you able to get video footage from the hotel awhile back?"

"Already on it, Eugeena."

"You are good, Detective Jones." Being married to a retired homicide detective had its perks.

I started clearing the table. "Did you hear anything interesting from my classmates you interviewed?"

"Not much more than what you have been telling me. Georgia wasn't a very well-liked person. Some of your classmates mentioned that her friend Pauline was one of the few people who could tolerate her. Which I have to say I don't get."

I waved my hand. "Pauline was just that kind of person. You know, the type that would take in the most difficult stray cats and dogs. She was always optimistic and for as long as I could remember, she served as class president. Some people just have it together and can get along with anyone."

"Mmmm. I guess. Seems like Georgia was a really complex person. Anyway, we will get some answers soon. Like I said, I'm waiting on the hotel footage."

"Oh, was it the same guy you worked with before?"

"No, this was a new guy. I believe Rosemary put in a word for us." Amos winked. "I think he may be sweet on her, too. He was more than happy to supply us with the video once we told him it was for Rosemary."

"You don't say." I thought about earlier today. "Rosemary seemed to perk up when I asked. What's this man's name?"

"Is it important?"

I looked at Amos. "Yes! Rosemary has been single for a decade. She raised her daughter, and now is helping her daughter raise her granddaughter. I'm happy to hear she's showing interest in someone."

Amos shook his head. "You're trying to solve a murder and play matchmaker. His name is Earl. Earl Anderson."

"Earl Anderson? Wait, I know him."

"You do?" Amos raised an eyebrow.

"They were all good friends, Rosemary's husband, Earl, and Jimmy."

"Sounds like your classmates are a lot more close-knit than you have described to me."

"I guess I hadn't thought about it. I haven't kept in touch with everyone. Rosemary lives in the neighborhood and we go to the same church, but we all have very separate lives."

"Well, if Earl was sweet on Rosemary back then, that hasn't changed." Amos turned to Porgy, who'd been snoring in the corner, oblivious to our conversation as usual. "Hey, Porgy, come on, buddy. I'm going to go out here and walk this chicken off in the yard."

He leaned over and kissed me on the cheek. "Don't worry, Eugeena. We will get to the bottom of all this."

Through the window over the sink, I watched Porgy and Amos walk across the yard. I felt blessed and grateful for both my male companions, the human and canine.

I wished happiness for my friend Rosemary as well. Even more so, I wished this business with Georgia would quickly be resolved.

Amos returned with Porgy trotting over to inspect his food bowl. In a few seconds, the sounds of crunching and grunting reverberated across the kitchen.

"All that dog does is sleep and eat." I glanced over at Amos, who peered down intently at his phone. I suspected Amos needed his reading glasses. "Are you able to see that screen? You are doing an awful lot of squinting."

He waved his hand. "Earl sent the footage. I'm just trying to scroll through it on this phone. I think I'm going to transfer this to the laptop."

"Good. I want to see the footage. I want to know exactly what happened when Georgia left."

And I didn't want to be squinting.

I followed Amos into his office/man cave. The room used to be a former office for my first husband, but it looked totally different. Ralph Patterson was a man of exquisite tastes who liked his art and John Coltrane.

Amos was more of a sporty guy. There were large posters of his favorite figures: Muhammad Ali, Michael Jordan, and Jackie Robinson. I always thought seniors were less tech-savvy, but Amos wasn't bad with a computer. He insisted on having two large monitors, something I'd never had before.

I had asked Amos if he was going to get a PI license, but he didn't seem interested. I don't know why. When he wasn't off fishing, he spent time on cases with his two buddies. Amos' former co-workers, Joe Douglas and Lenny Wilkes, had become official PIs after they retired.

They worked out of Joe's home, who was the only bachelor in the crew. The last time I visited, Joe had the front room decked out like an office with a whiteboard in the corner.

Before pressing play, Amos turned to me. "Are you sure you really want to know?"

"Of course, I do. And it's all so odd. I can't let go that someone is purposely trying to set up Rosemary."

"Alright, here goes."

I peered at the screen and pointed. "That's Georgia and Jimmy in the elevator. I don't believe Georgia is listening to a word he's saying."

Jimmy loomed behind Georgia as she marched off the elevator through the lobby on a mission. I watched as they both exited outside. There was another couple entering the hotel. They swerved around Georgia, but she still bumped into a young man dressed in a burgundy blazer and khakis. The young man stared at Georgia with his hands up.

Not acknowledging him, Georgia instead spun around and held her bony finger up near Jimmy's face. He stepped back and crossed his arms, like nothing she was telling him was new.

I watched Jimmy's face. He appeared solemn at first, but then his eyes flashed, and his mouth turned down like he had been fed up with Georgia. He spun around and left her with her hands gesturing. Georgia stood there for a moment, peering inside the sliding doors before turning around.

"Wow!" I said after a few seconds. "That was intense. I wonder what they were talking about. Do you think anyone heard them?"

Amos nodded and pointed to the screen. "We're attempting to track down the young valet that Georgia almost knocked over. Let me hit rewind. You will see that he had to have heard the conversation."

I watched the screen speed backward. When Amos

stopped the video, I shook my head as Georgia stomped outside like a bull ready to run over anyone in her way. Amos paused on the young man as he looked wide-eyed at Georgia and Jimmy. "I guess that wasn't something he saw every day. So, when does Georgia come back in and why?"

Amos answered. "I don't know why yet, but she comes back about ten minutes later. I'm going to fast forward. Look at the time in the corner, Eugeena."

I leaned forward on the chair and watched as Georgia entered the hotel lobby again. "It is about ten minutes. She has her phone in her hand and she keeps looking down at it. Could someone be texting her?"

Amos chimed in. "Yeah, that's what I think."

"So someone lured her back inside." I looked over at Amos. "I don't suppose you all are high-tech enough to get her phone records?"

He shook his head. "That's going to be hard, not to include illegal. Chris did volunteer to help, but I don't want him to get into trouble with Wilkes."

"I agree. The problem is, I have a feeling this will connect back to Rosemary. Remember, someone stole her badge and her phone."

"This is all sounds premeditated."

I hoped we were both wrong.

"If this is the case, I don't know how far in advance this person had this idea. Georgia wasn't even on the list to come. Maybe they decided when she showed up and was arguing with Rosemary. Still, it makes little sense why they would shift the crime to appear like Rosemary did it."

"She has to have some enemies."

"That's the other problem. The one enemy we are sure of was the one who wound up dead in her office. There's someone else in the picture." I turned back to the big screen. "Are there no other exits? You can't see anyone in the hallway."

Amos shook his head. "The hotel invests in surveillance mainly around the entrances and exits. There are cameras around and inside the elevators. I guess to protect employee's privacy, there are no cameras around the office area. Now, there are some cameras on the floors, but there are none inside the ballrooms, just around the elevators and the hallway. It's expensive to keep all this footage on the server and the hotel wouldn't want their guests to be made nervous by cameras."

"It would be like big brother watching. So, we're limited to seeing who came and went from the ballroom." I crossed my arms. "Would the person have gotten some evidence on them? They hit Georgia on the head. Remember, she had that gash on her head. Any ideas on the weapon?"

Amos answered. "I'm thinking it would have been something in Rosemary's office, like a paperweight. The person could have left that room with some evidence on their clothes. They also could have left some trace evidence too." He pointed to the screen. "Wilkes may have to rely on any evidence the techs gathered. The camera isn't helpful. There must be some exit we don't know about."

"Mmm." Well, I knew we would not get access to evidence. That's when a thought occurred to me based on what Amos said.

My thoughts must have been written all over my face; Amos asked. "What now, Eugeena? Please tell me that look doesn't mean what I think it means."

I wasn't about to confess the potential trouble I could stir up. I already knew Amos would try to talk me out of it.

Instead, I stood to leave his office. "Nothing. I just need to reach out to Rosemary about something."

Now if only I could convince Rosemary to go along with the idea.

Lord, please help keep me out of trouble.

Chapter 10

"You want to do what?" Rosemary exclaimed.

It was good that I called her on the phone. I'm sure she would've wanted to knock me out if we were in-person. A person can only be but so nice, and I knew Rosemary had her limits.

I took a deep breath and tried to convince her again. "The hotel cameras don't extend to your office area, Rosemary. Georgia went off-camera at a certain point. I feel like someone is trying to purposely set you up. I want to see your office layout and if you remember anything."

My plan was to go to the hotel and figure out how Georgia could have been killed. When I was a teacher, I did situations with my students all the time, like mock trials or mock votes. It helped bring home the learning and kept students engaged. The footage Amos shared only convinced me that the killer knew exactly who he or she was doing and made a clean getaway.

But how? I needed to know.

It took more persuasion, mainly begging, but Rosemary finally agreed. She knew Charleston Place Hotel better than anybody. She'd worked there for twenty-five years.

To keep things simple, I rode over to the hotel with

Rosemary, but I wondered if I should have been the driver. I could tell by the way Rosemary gripped the steering wheel she was nervous.

I asked her for the tenth time. "Are you sure you want to do this? I forgot you're not supposed to be in the building."

Rosemary said, "That's not really true. Mr. Montague just wanted me to take a bit of a break. He didn't say I shouldn't be on the premises."

"You still seem nervous."

"Not about going to the hotel, okay? Well, maybe I am. I haven't been in my office since we found Georgia."

"I know. We don't have to do this." I think I needed an excuse to chicken out myself. I hadn't even told Amos what I was doing.

That can't be good!

"Eugeena, you have me thinking now. How did someone get my access key, lure Georgia into my office, kill her and get out of the hotel without being noticed?"

"In any cop show I've ever seen, they would not have gotten away without getting something on them or leaving something of them behind. That's way above our heads and we can only pray Wilkes finds something. This person was able to get around cameras. They would have to have some knowledge of the hotel, just like you."

"I guess. I just can't think of anyone I work with doing this. And to plan this out. No one we know is that much of a mastermind."

We both remained quiet in our own thoughts. I didn't want to voice out loud what else I was thinking. I still wondered if Rosemary was in some type of danger. None of it made sense.

It was after six o'clock when Rosemary and I entered

the Charleston Place hotel. Instead of entering through the lobby, I followed Rosemary through a parking lot in the back, which had lines of signs that stated, "Parking for Charleston Place Hotel Employees Only."

I have to admit; it felt like we were creeping around. Daylight savings time was in a few weeks, but it was already getting dark earlier. The parking lot was fairly empty. Then I recalled Rosemary said she didn't receive another access key.

"How are you planning to get into the office?"

"Don't worry, I have a way in." She pulled out her phone and dialed a number. "Earl, this is Rosemary. Can you let me in?"

Earl? Oh, that, Earl.

Rosemary turned around and looked at me. "Why are you looking at me like that? You know Earl. He's friends with Jimmy."

"Oh, I know him. My question is how well do you know him? A smile that bright from you has been rare these past few weeks."

Rosemary giggled. "You need to stop. Earl and I have always been good friends."

"Mmmm."

A few minutes later, a man with a thick middle and skinny legs appeared at the door. Completely bald, dressed in a security uniform, Earl grinned when he saw Rosemary. When he opened the door, he boomed. "Hey, Rose."

Rose? Why was he shouting? Practically announcing our visit.

I took a quick glance around and didn't see anyone.

The only person I remember ever calling her Rose was her deceased husband. If we weren't about to be sneaking around the hotel, I would ask these two if they needed to get a room. Seeing that I was still a newlywed, I knew one was never too old to be enamored by love.

To confirm my suspicions, Rosemary turned on her 100-watt smile and purred. "Hey, Earl. You remember Eugeena."

"Yeah. Hey, Eugeena. I met your new husband, Amos, and his friend yesterday." He turned around to check behind him and then turned back. He whispered, "I hope that stuff was helpful."

I grinned, glad to see Rosemary had an ally here at the hotel. "Yes, it was very helpful. Do you mind if Rosemary and I walk around a bit? We need to put some things together."

Earl hiked up his britches at the waist. "Sure, y'all need any help with anything?"

"Yes," Rosemary cringed. "Is it possible to get in my office? Do you know if it's closed off?"

"I think it's open. I know a big cleaning crew was in most of the day yesterday and last night. A few people have been in. Most are working down the hall in another office or working remotely. Kind of weird not seeing people. I definitely miss seeing you around, Rose."

Earl sounded like a teenager pining away. The way Rose exchanged looks with him, she seemed to have lost some years from her face.

I hated to break up the two lovebirds, but I wanted to be in and out. "Can you be on the lookout for us, Earl? We shouldn't be too long."

"Absolutely, let me walk you down to the office, and then I need to get back to the control room."

The further we walked down the hall, the more I had second thoughts about this. Even if the cleaning crew had been in, I could still picture Georgia's body on the floor in my mind.

Beside me, Rosemary seemed to slow her pace as we neared the office.

I hooked my arm in hers. "We can do this, Rosemary."

Earl held his badge up to the panel next to the door. The door unlocked with a click and Earl pulled the door, swinging it open inside. "I can come in with you."

"No, no, you've done enough already. I can do this. Thank you so much, Earl."

He grinned. "Alright, holler if you need me."

After Earl trotted down the hallway, I looked back at Rosemary. "Ready?"

She nodded. "Let's do this."

When Rosemary pushed the door open, smells of bleach and some other scents hit my nose. "The cleaning crew definitely did their thing."

We shuffled into the office, and Rosemary hit a switch. Lights flickered across the ceiling. All the office doors were open, including the dreaded office we were about to enter.

Rosemary and I stood in the doorway as if crossing the threshold was more like trying to cross an ocean.

"The carpet is gone," Rosemary commented.

"Yeah, all your furniture seems to be pushed to the side. Do you really think you can come back in here to work?"

"I've been thinking about it, and I'm not really sure. I'm kind of enjoy being at home and being there when Amani arrives home from school. Michelle likes that one of us can cook real home-cooked dinners for a change. You seem to have blossomed in your retirement life."

"It's had its moments. Let's think this through so we can be in and out. I don't want you or Earl to get into any trouble." I pulled out my phone.

"What do you have there?"

"The hotel footage."

"Let me see."

I showed her my phone. We watched as Georgia left and then argued with Jimmy before turning around.

"Looks like she insulted Jimmy. I'm grateful he went after her, but it did little good."

I agreed. "No, it didn't. See, here she comes back with her phone in her hand."

"She's texting someone." Rosemary squinted at the phone. "Then she goes off to the right. Well, that's the general direction of our offices."

"Yep, she comes here but never leaves. So someone took your badge. Georgia didn't have it on her, but the killer did."

Rosemary shuddered. "I'm getting the heebie jeebies now, Eugeena."

"We will make this quick. So they have to hold the badge up to the bar next to the panel by the door. When we arrived to put your punch bowl in the office, the door was open."

"Yes, someone stuck a doorstop inside the door." Rosemary stated.

"So the door was already open for Georgia to just walk in. And your door was open, so she assumed that was where to go."

"Someone was pretending to be me."

I swallowed. "I'm afraid so."

"But why?"

I shook my head. "I know we all like to believe everyone loves us, but ... One thing at a time. So someone had to have been to your office to know its location. I remember when we were planning the reception for Carmen and

Cedric's wedding, I came to your office. Do you have other clients come to your office?"

She nodded. "People come to my office to fill out paperwork and sign contracts for reserving the ballrooms."

"Would any of these people see you using your key card to get into the office? We need to get that list of people and narrow it down. Let's start with the fact the person had to have known Georgia. Did any of our classmates go to your office?"

"Yes, I'm not sure why I didn't think of this before. No one has asked, but people from the committee have been in my office. I had a couple of them come by since I started keeping some reunion-related materials in my office."

Now we're getting somewhere.

"Okay, so who was on the committee? We should have done this in the first place."

"Well, Claudia was on the committee."

"How are things with you and Claudia?"

"We were never really friends in school. She's changed a lot, a lot more outgoing. She had really good ideas about how things were set up. I can't say we talked much over the years."

"Who else is on the committee?"

"Well, Sharise was on the committee."

I slapped myself upside the head. "They were both on the committee and both in your office?"

"Yes. Why?"

"You remember when they came to the restroom to talk about Georgia."

"That doesn't mean they did anything to her." Rosemary looked at me. "Right?"

"It's mighty suspicious. Although I have to say I didn't

get a I killed my classmate vibe when I talked to Claudia. Sharise displayed the most venom."

"You're so right. But, Eugeena, it's hard to believe anyone we went to school with would go to this length to kill Georgia. She must have really done something this time. There were so many times when I wanted to—"

A shrill voice interrupted Rosemary and had us both jumping out of our skin.

"What are you doing in here?"

Chapter 11

A tall, imposing woman stood in the doorway of the main office staring at me and Rosemary. She stepped forward, as if walking unsteadily on stilts.

I peered down at the stilettos she worked. They had to be six inches.

"Should you even be here?" she asked sharply.

Rosemary looked at me and then turned to the woman. "I still work here, Catalina."

Oh, so this was Catalina Montague. She appeared older than I imagined when Rosemary first mentioned her. Her long legs were barely covered by the shirtdress she wore, and the distinction around her lips and cheeks spoke Botox to me. It was a shame. She was a pretty woman, just aging. Despite her age, she was dressed as if she'd just come off a runway.

Catalina swung her icy blond hair to the side. "I know that. I just thought after finding your friend murdered in your office, this would be the last place you would be."

"She was a classmate, not my friend."

I didn't like where this conversation was going and wanted to know why this person showed up when we were here. It was after work hours. "Rosemary, this is?" I thought introductions were needed.

Rosemary grimaced. "Catalina, this is my friend, Eugeena. Eugeena, this is Catalina Montague. Her uncle owns the Charleston Place Hotel."

Catalina quirked her eyebrow. "Hello, Eugeena. Rosemary, it's unnecessary to introduce me that way. People already think I haven't earned my place here, but I work hard too."

"Of course you do." Rosemary appeased. "Why are you here so late? I came by to check on my office, which has been thoroughly cleaned."

Catalina waved her hand across her nose. "Yes, I don't know if it will really help. Many people are having trouble coming in here to work."

"What about you?" I asked. "Were you here the night the hotel hosted our high school reunion?"

Catalina looked at me as if I was something odd that she wished she hadn't seen. "I don't know why you are asking me that; Rosemary knows I wasn't here."

"I do? Why wouldn't you have been here?" Rosemary said.

Catalina frowned. "I went on a trip the Friday before your reunion. My boyfriend whisked me off to Saint Maarten for the weekend. In fact, he gave me this." She held up her hand in front of us.

After I got past the bony fingers, I saw the large, bright sparkling diamond. "Wow," I exclaimed. "Somebody loves you."

Catalina giggled like a schoolgirl. "Yes, he does. I'm so excited. I'm here to pick up some things. I've already given my uncle my two weeks' notice, but I insisted I'm allowed to work remotely. Not really hard to convince him with all that has gone on."

"You're leaving?" Rosemary commented. "I thought you wanted... that you had plans to move up here in this hotel."

Catalina stared at Rosemary like she had grown bored. "I did. But now I have new plans. My boyfriend owns a resort down at Saint Maarten, and I get to be a manager."

Rosemary and I exchanged looks. Her thoughts about Catalina trying to boot her out of her job seemed to fade into the wind.

"Oh. Well, I'm thrilled for you." Rosemary smiled.

We stood around watching Catalina open the door to her office. She rifled around in some drawers for a few minutes before stepping out. She walked past us before remembering we were there. Frowning, she asked, "Oh, are you going to lock up, Rosemary?"

"Of course, I will make sure the office is locked."

"Great. Sad about your friend again."

Instead of going out the door we entered, Catalina went around the corner to another exit. I hadn't noticed it before.

Rosemary placed her hands on her hips and huffed. "She wasn't my friend."

All we saw was the woman's retreating back that appeared to be heading out into the parking lot.

I commented. "You can put your daughter's fears to rest about your co-worker. That woman doesn't have a care in the world other than she's about to be a bride."

Rosemary sighed. "Yeah, I agree. I really didn't think she was after my job or anything. As you just saw, she's kind of into herself and wants to be important."

"No worries about her anymore." I looked back and forth for a few minutes.

Rosemary asked. "What are you thinking about?"

"I didn't realize that exit was there. How come we came in through the side public entrance?"

"The public entrance connects to the guests' keycards so they can access their rooms by entering from the back parking lot. Employee badges are different. You have to have an employee badge to enter the door back there and as you know I don't have one."

I walked towards the door and pushed it open. Just as I opened it, a white Porsche came speeding past us. "I'm assuming that's Catalina."

"You assumed correctly. I don't even know why the woman bothers to work. Her family is filthy rich."

"Mmmm." I peered down at the door. "Rosemary, when I came to your office a year ago, you didn't show me out this door. I went all the way out into the hallway to exit."

"It's really not a door that anyone from the public sees. Although, I exited through this door last week. Claudia and Sharise were in my office. Eugeena, I'm getting old. I didn't think about this. Is this important?"

"I don't know, but I have a feeling this was a good getaway point for the killer. It still disturbs me; there had to be time for some planning. We're going to have to talk to Claudia and Sharise at some point."

Rosemary wrinkled her nose. "I didn't get bad vibes from either of them. I have a hard time seeing them go to this extent to kill Georgia. And why involve me?"

"That's what we need to find out."

Chapter 12

On the drive back, Rosemary got cold feet about talking to Claudia and Sharise. I reminded her. "You didn't have a problem talking to Jimmy."

"That's different. It's Jimmy. I've known him all my life and..."

"And what?"

"I don't know if you remember this, but Jimmy and I were boyfriend and girlfriend for like a minute."

I frowned. "I don't remember that; it must have been like seconds. In fact, I only remember when Jimmy started dating Georgia. I was thankful because she kept giving me the evil eye every time she saw me with Ralph."

"I forgot she dated Ralph. Oh, yeah. She was furious with you. I have to say, I was glad she wasn't paying attention to me. Anyway, I dated Jimmy around the time you started dating Ralph."

I held up my hand. "Okay, my head is spinning now. How is it we were all dating the same people?"

"We had a small school, and we were all tight. People got upset with each other and their feelings were hurt for a while, but it was all puppy love."

"Unless you wound up pregnant like me."

"Oh, come on. You still loved Ralph though."

"I did. But for a while there, he didn't want me after I got pregnant. I believe he only changed his tune when my father got involved. Then he did the right thing."

My marriage to Ralph wasn't easy, but our remaining years together were a pleasant change.

Now, my second marriage was the sweetest thing in my life.

Rosemary pulled in front of our house. "Eugeena, I appreciate you helping me."

"I don't know if we accomplished anything, but we crossed one suspect off the list."

Rosemary cringed. "I really never thought Catalina was a threat to me. Just one of those overbearing people who was related to the owner."

"That makes life difficult. I will call Claudia after the funeral tomorrow."

Rosemary looked at me. "You're going to Georgia's funeral?"

Earlier this week, I would have pondered if it was a good idea to attend Georgia's funeral. Funerals to me were for people who would truly love and miss the person. It provided an opportunity to mourn. Even if she had never been my favorite person, I felt bad about the way Georgia died. It may have had something to do with our lunch conversation with Jimmy. Somehow, I saw Georgia for the first time, beyond the messy life that she led.

I finally spoke my thoughts out loud. "If we don't go to her funeral, people are going to talk more. You already feel like people are suspicious about us."

"We did nothing wrong."

"I agree. But we can show people we have nothing to hide."

"You have a valid point, Eugeena. I will meet you at the church."

I squeezed my friend's hand. "It will be alright. You'll see." I reached for the door handle and climbed out of her car. "Sleep well."

Rosemary grimaced. "I'll try. Pray for me, Sister."

It wasn't until I watched Rosemary's taillights fade away that I realized how late it was. When I entered the house, an irate voice said, "Eugeena, where have you been?"

I clutched my chest as if a bullet had shot me. Amos was sitting in the living room with only the faint glow of the television. He switched on the lamp beside the couch and stared at me like I had done something wrong.

"Amos, you scared the mess out of me."

"Why should you be scared? Were you doing something you had no business, Eugeena? It's after nine o'clock."

Heat rose in my chest and into my cheeks. "What's up with your accusatory tone? I wasn't doing anything wrong."

Amos raised an eyebrow. "Well, you are looking kind of guilty about something. Why are you all defensive?"

I took a deep breath. This wasn't going in a good direction. Something obviously upset Amos, and I was about to blow my top. It may have had something to do with the fact that I was used to doing my own thing. When I was married to Ralph, there was no questioning in our relationship. Ralph was always at the hospital, and I was always the one tending to the children. The children and I went to church, to school and a lot of times we didn't see Ralph until dinner time, if that.

"I'm sorry. You have nothing to worry about. I was with Rosemary and we went back to the hotel to check out some things."

"You could have told me. Why were you at the hotel? The office is still a crime scene."

"The crime scene cleaners already cleaned the office."

"I see," Amos said, still appearing perturbed. "It still would have been nice to know where you were. You have a tendency to get into trouble, just in case you forgot past incidents."

He had a point. I went off and found myself in interesting situations. The last one had me almost looking at death's door. The crazy thing was it wasn't the first time that happened. I was grateful to God for looking out for me, sending his angels, one being my husband who always seemed to know when I was about to dive headfirst into trouble.

My anger subsided. Amos and I had not been married a full year yet. While we disagreed over things like Amos forgetting to put the toilet seat down or the pile of clothes he sometimes left on the floor... Why men did that, I didn't know. I'd had my share of picking up clothes after two boys and Ralph. But other than that, we really didn't disagree on a lot of things.

I could sense tension building in Amos. He sighed as if he didn't know what to do with me. "I don't know how many times I have to tell you this. You don't have any training for going after a killer."

"I'm not going after a killer," my voice rose.

Amos raised an eyebrow. "Are you sure? What was the reason you went back to the hotel?"

I held my head down. "I know you and my family get worried about me. When I taught in the classroom, I had a healthy curiosity about history. History repeats itself. It's important to learn from what happened in the past."

I sat down next to Amos. "I think because

these situations have dropped into my lap, it triggers my curiosity about the person and their past. I don't need to tell you, you already know. This was your career for over thirty years, but something in the victim's past, even if it was just the immediate past, points to the reason they were killed. And this feels like an obvious setup."

Amos added. "And you have a history with Georgia. Plus, you've seen how she's rubbed many people the wrong way over the years. You're curious about who she pushed past the point of no return."

"That's right. There are many people who could have killed her." I grabbed my notebook and told Amos about Claudia and Sharise.

He eyed me. "Is it really a good idea for you to talk to them?"

"I won't be alone, and we will meet in public like I told you."

He looked at my list. "I see you crossed Catalina Montague off your list."

"Oh, we saw her at the hotel tonight. Believe me, she is not a suspect and no threat to Rosemary. She's too busy showing off her huge diamond ring and ready to move to Saint Maarten in the Caribbean."

"Okay, what about Jimmy?"

I frowned. "He's planning his ex-wife's funeral. Have you ever heard of such a thing?"

"No, I haven't, which makes it suspicious to me."

"You ate the man's chicken earlier today. He runs a reputable business and has moved on with a new wife. What would be his motive?"

"I'm looking into some things. Just be wary."

I heard what Amos was saying, but Jimmy was not a point of interest to me.

"You know, I learned more about Georgia when we talked to him yesterday. It's completely true when they say hurt people hurt other people. Now I feel sorry for a person who I didn't understand."

"That's understandable, but there is still someone out there who killed her. Any murder is pretty scary, but when a person thinks about it, that's even scarier. I just want you to be careful and let me know what you're doing. I'm not trying to be a control freak. I just know how people are in this world."

I leaned over and hugged him. I did not want to upset the balance of our new marriage. Gratefulness flooded me. God knew to send me someone special who had the experience and also the gumption to tell me about myself.

"I appreciate you. Let's try not to go to bed angry."

He smiled. "I'm not angry. Just concerned. I'm not trying to lose my woman."

"I have no intentions of going anywhere, Mr. Jones. Now I think it's time we made up."

Chapter 13

I stayed off my sleuthing until the funeral. Amos' worry had clamped down some of my curiosities. Though I wondered if Claudia and Sharise would be at the funeral today. My suspicions were raised by the peculiar friendship between them and Georgia. And they both were privy to Rosemary's office location.

We walked into Missionary Baptist in the middle of the day on Friday, and I was surprised by the number of our classmates who still lived in Charleston that were in attendance. Although most of us were retired, I suspected some other attendees, like Annie Mae and Willie Mae, were there out of curiosity. I gave the twins the eye but continued down the aisle towards the open casket in front of the church.

Amos decided not to walk up with us and saved us some seats.

Rosemary and I peered down together over Georgia's casket.

I commented. "She looks good."

"Almost peaceful," Rosemary agreed.

We turned around to find Jimmy and his wife, Florida

in the front pew. I was glad Jimmy had moved on and remarried. I hoped he would be at peace, too.

We found our way back to our seats, and I scooted over next to Amos. Soon, several pastors entered the pulpit, including Pastor Jones. As usual with these funerals, Pastor Jones preached long and had many good things to say about Georgia. There was an art, I imagined, to talk about an individual who didn't fare well with other people.

After the funeral, we drove out to the graveyard. We stood at a distance as Pastor Jones spoke the final eulogy over Georgia's casket. I felt someone at my elbow before turning around to find Detective Wilkes.

"Detective, nice to see you."

The young woman smiled at me. "I'm surprised you all came to the funeral."

Rosemary looked as offended as I felt. "We weren't close friends with Georgia, but she was a classmate."

The detective shrugged. "I thought maybe it would be difficult for you to come to the funeral."

"We didn't get along with her," Rosemary said, "but we are Christian women. It's the right thing to do."

Wilkes nodded. "Yes. I think it's admirable."

Did she? I detected some sarcasm from Detective Wilkes.

In fact, I could almost see the wheels turning in her head. I commented. "You know, I watch crime shows and read a lot of crime books. I know what you're thinking."

The detective looked at me with a raised eyebrow. "I didn't realize you were a mind reader, Ms. Eugeena. What am I thinking?"

"I know most law enforcement think the killer shows up at the funeral."

"That's often true." Wilkes agreed.

"Is that why you're here?"

"I do like to look around, check to see who showed up. Make notes."

I looked around the gravesite again, this time more deliberately, to see if I could detect what Detective Wilkes observed. There was Jimmy. Claudia. Sharise. In high school, the same group of people gravitated toward each other. The group had aged, now with some missing members.

Georgia, Claudia, Sharise and Pauline.

Two out of four.

"What was that?"

I turned to find Detective Wilkes eyeing me closely. I frowned. "Sorry?"

"You said two out of four. What did you mean?"

I didn't realize I'd said anything out loud. "Just thinking about the four friends. Pauline died two years ago. She was the bubbly one in the group. Now Georgia is gone. Only Claudia and Sharise remain."

"Interesting observation," she quipped.

"This was our forty-fifth high school reunion. You asked why we were here. A lot of our classmates aren't here. When you get to be this age, and you're still around, it's a time of humility and gratitude. We don't know what will happen tomorrow.

"Very true! Thank you for your insights as always, Ms. Eugeena. I will be in touch."

We watched her walked away.

Rosemary looked at me. "What did she mean? I will be in touch. Why does that sound ominous?"

"That's Detective Wilkes for you. Probably her way of saying that we're not out of the woods yet." I watched the detective make her way over to Claudia and Sharise.

Rosemary twisted her hands. "Georgia was in my office. Do you think I should get a lawyer? Do you have the name of the lawyer who worked with Carmen last year?"

"Yes, I do. It may not hurt to have him on speed dial. But still. I don't know what she could do to pin anything on you or me. We were oblivious to the fact that Georgia would have been in your office."

"You're right. But they have to pin down a suspect. You know what? I don't feel good. I've done my duty today. I paid my respects to a woman who didn't like me very much. I'm going to head home. I need some time to think before Michelle and Amani arrive home."

I hugged Rosemary. "Take care of yourself."

"You too, Eugeena. We will get through this."

I glanced over at Jimmy and noticed that Detective Wilkes had moved over to where he stood with his wife. The detective said something to him. I watched his face, which had been somber. Observing people had been something I picked up during my time as a schoolteacher. It paid to pay attention and listen to your students. While I taught everyone the same lesson, each student had their own personality and comprehension skill.

What I remembered about my eighth graders, they were not good at hiding their emotions. Some adults over time learned the skill. It was important to keep your emotions in check for certain situations like your job, in public, and at church. These days, someone's phone could film you. My mama used to tell me to fix my face. In fact, she always told me that. To this day, I have not learned.

Across from me, I watched Jimmy's face morph into an angry mask marring his handsome looks. The detective left him standing there. That's when I noticed his clenched fists. His wife rubbed his shoulder as if she could remove the tension from his body.

Amos walked up beside me and noticed where I was staring.

He commented. "Jimmy Hayes doesn't look too happy."

"No. I wonder what the detective said to him."

"Probably that she's monitoring him. You and Rosemary might have found Georgia, which places you under suspicion, but as far as all the witnesses have recalled, Jimmy was still the last person we know to see Georgia alive."

"But he planned her funeral. He probably still loves her even though he moved on with a new wife. There was history between them. A dead son."

"Love makes you do funny things, Eugeena. From what I have gathered from some of your classmates, Jimmy and Georgia had a pretty contentious relationship."

I peered at Amos. "Given Georgia's nature, I'm not surprised."

Amos nodded. "I haven't briefed you about what me and the fellas found. There were a few domestic violence house calls from both of them."

"From both of them?"

"Yes, Georgia called the cops on Jimmy. But there were a few calls that went the other way."

I raised an eyebrow. "Jimmy called the cops on her?"

"Yes."

"That I can believe. I remember Georgia getting into physical fights when we were younger. I'm sorry, Amos. Jimmy has always been a good guy. I'm not saying he didn't lay hands on her, but I guess people can be pushed past their limits of tolerance. Georgia did that to a lot of people."

"Yeah, I'm sure that's on Detective Wilkes' mind. At least when I was on a case, that would have kept him as a suspect for me."

"Well, I hate to say this, but as long as Wilkes keeps me and Rosemary off her list, I can't complain. Let's head home."

As Amos and I made our way out of the gravesite, I took a moment to look back. Jimmy was standing off by himself. I remembered him saying that Georgia wanted to be buried beside their son. I wondered how he felt having his first family completely gone.

There was no denying he was the last person seen with Georgia. Could Jimmy harbor enough bitterness towards his ex-wife that finally came to a violent end?

As Amos drove us back to the house, I wondered if I'd misjudged Jimmy.

Chapter 14

On Saturday, I opened the door of Sugar Creek Cafe, one of my favorite places. But even the aroma of the coffee beans didn't lift my mood. My mind was still on the funeral and Amos's information about Jimmy and Georgia's domestic confrontations. I could see why the detective would have her eye on him.

This whole thing was really making me wonder about my ability to read people. I had been wrong before, sometimes, not paying attention to the red flags waving in front of my face.

It also didn't help that Rosemary didn't want to join me for this interview. My friend, who usually remained optimistic, appeared to be having a hard time. This made me even more determined to understand Georgia's death. Still keeping my promise to Amos to meet in public places, I moved ahead with my coffee meeting with Claudia.

When I looked around the cafe, I didn't see her. Sugar Creek Cafe looked part coffeehouse and also like an extended family room. The front half of the cafe had booths around the walls and tables in the middle. I wondered if Claudia was towards the back, where the decor consisted of couches, comfy big chairs, and coffee tables.

I stood in a short line and perused the menu even though I knew what I wanted. When I reached the counter, I smiled when greeted by a familiar face. My next-door neighbor, Jocelyn Miller, grinned back at me. I noticed her badge name and quirked my eyebrow at her. "Joss."

"Hey, Ms. Eugeena. Yeah, I asked my boss if I could change my name tag. Everyone calls me that anyway, even my grandmother."

"Okay, I didn't know that. It sounds cute, and it fits you." Joss lived with her grandmother, my longtime neighbor, Louise Hopkins. For a while, her now deceased son had placed Louise in a nursing home, even though she was sharp as she could be despite being in her seventies. Through bittersweet circumstances, Louise lost her only son but found the daughter she gave up for adoption years ago. Joss seemed to have developed more of a relationship with her grandmother than her mother, but I knew things were improving.

Joss leaned forward and asked in a low voice. "Are you okay? My grandmother and I saw the news. Was that your high school reunion?"

"Yes, that was one of my classmates."

Joss nodded. "We thought so. I know you are probably on the case. Any suspects?"

I chuckled. "No, but I will keep you and Louise apprised of my findings." Somehow, my activities also sparked other amateur sleuthing between my family and close friends. This was not a hobby I would recommend to anyone, but I appreciated the support I received.

Joss prompted me. "Will you have your usual today, Ms. Eugeena?"

"Yes, a coffee with two Splendas and cream is fine."

I stood to the side to wait for my coffee. I turned when the front entrance door jingled. Claudia glided inside. The woman's walk reminded me of a supermodel strutting down a catwalk.

Funny thing, I couldn't remember Claudia being this eloquent when we were in school. I remembered her being homely, the kind of person you forget was standing next to you. She'd blended in back then, but now she stood out. We all changed over the years, but some were more obvious than others.

"Eugeena, how are you?" Claudia glanced around. "Sorry, I'm late. Is Rosemary here?"

"Unfortunately, Rosemary's not feeling well today. This has been a traumatic time for her."

"I can imagine." Claudia held her hand to her chest as if to stop her heart palpitations. "It has been stressful for all of us, but I heard you two found Georgia. You must be affected by this too."

I smiled. She was right. Georgia's untimely death had disrupted my life, which I had been trying to keep normal.

"Ms. Eugeena, your coffee is ready," Joss said.

I turned and picked up the cup, placing my hand around the brown wrapper. "Thank you, Joss. Claudia, how about I get us a table in the back?"

She nodded. "That will be wonderful." Claudia stepped up to the counter. "Honey, I would like a caramel latte."

As Claudia waited for her order, I walked to the back. I located an area that included two sitting chairs with a tall round table between them. On either side of the chairs were bookshelves filled with books, some classics and other more modern authors.

The owner of Sugar Creek Cafe was a former student of mine. I admired her taste, which had always been eclectic even as a child. I settled into the high-back chair and sipped my coffee, blowing on it occasionally, until Claudia rounded the corner.

She sat down in the opposite chair, facing me. "This is nice. It's a shame we haven't gotten together before."

"Yes, I'm sorry." I wasn't sure why I was apologizing; Claudia and I weren't friends in high school. More like acquaintances. We had a small high school class, and we all knew each other, mainly because we journeyed through the younger grades together.

"Did you attend Georgia's funeral?" Claudia asked before taking a sip of her latte.

"Yes, I did. I saw you with Sharise and Jimmy. A lot of your group has passed on."

"Yes, you're right. Pauline was an enormous loss."

I lifted an eyebrow. "Just Pauline?"

Claudia looked sheepish. "I know this conversation is about Georgia, but Pauline kept us together. Sharise couldn't stand Georgia because of the way she'd bullied her when they were younger, but Pauline kept the peace. I don't know how she did it. She'd always been good-natured and positive. Loved the Lord. She found out she had stage four ovarian cancer, but she didn't fret or complain, at least not around any of us."

We remained silent. I remembered Pauline's bubbly personality, always with a smile and eyes that sparkled.

I interrupted our quiet reverie. "At the reunion, would you say Georgia's acting out was her way of expressing how much she missed Pauline?"

Claudia wiped delicately at her nose with a napkin. "Georgia had her issues, but she loved Pauline like a sister."

"Any thoughts on what happened last Saturday?"

Claudia squirmed a bit. "I've thought of nothing else. I'm scared of my thoughts."

I scooted higher in the seat. "Why? Do you have some ideas about who did this?"

"Well, everyone saw her leave with Jimmy. She complained about him, but she was kind of codependent on him, too. They would be separated a few years and then back together again."

"Codependent? So they took a long time to get a divorce?"

Claudia nodded. "Jimmy always was good to Georgia. He tried to deal with her foolish behavior. I heard when he asked for a divorce, she wouldn't sign the papers. He was ready to move on with Florida but Georgia dragged her feet."

I frowned. "I heard they had some domestic calls during their marriage. Seems like Jimmy would have cut her loose a long time ago."

Claudia pursed her lips. "I agree. But as far as I know, he never hit her. I can't say the same for Georgia; she had anger issues and would pick fights. Kind of like she did at the reunion. People didn't know she regretted her outbursts, though. Even showed remorse, but she rarely apologized. When she was married to Jimmy, I think she didn't like competing with the Chicken Shack. After his dad passed, Jimmy really threw himself into building up the Chicken Shack as a restaurant chain."

"He has to have become wealthy over the years."

"You're right! Jimmy slaved over the business to please

his father. He wanted to make the business his own. Bigger and better. Anyway regardless of his success, Georgia was forever going to be tied to Jimmy because of Jason."

"I can see that." I commented. "Jason was their only child."

"You know, when he died last year, I've never seen Jimmy and Georgia closer. Usually, when a child dies, it drives the parents apart. They had already been apart for a couple of years. But getting Jason to do better was always their combined mission."

I leaned forward. "It's all very tragic. With Jimmy being one of the last people to see her alive, I would have liked to have been a fly on the wall after they left the reunion."

Claudia puckered her lips. She appeared as if she had something else to say, but then kept quiet.

I narrowed my eyes, wondering if this woman had anything to hide. She knew more about Georgia and Jimmy's life than I originally thought. I changed the conversation to see if I could get her talking in a new direction.

"Tell me more about you, Claudia. I think I remember you saying you wanted to be a lawyer."

She smiled. "Yes, I've been a lawyer all these years. Not a criminal lawyer, just a business lawyer. I specialize in corporate law."

"Wonderful." I frowned. "Was your husband at the reunion?"

"No," her voice faltered. "My husband passed four years ago. I married later in life and my husband was much older than me. We didn't have kids. Funny thing, he was one of my clients. A local business owner."

"Oh, I'm so sorry. I understand about widowhood. I experienced that until, well, earlier this year. Amos and I married this past February."

Claudia beamed. "I'm so happy for you, Eugeena. I remember when you and Ralph dated. It's good you could find love again, especially at our age."

I commented. "I'm not the only one. Jimmy did too."

Claudia held her hand over her mouth as she laughed. "That's right. I would never say this in front of Georgia, but Florida seemed better for him."

I chuckled. "Probably because she's a lot younger."

"You noticed that too. Sharise adores her. She says Florida has brought a lot of changes to the Chicken Shack and she's been good for Jimmy. You know, until the funeral, I didn't realize how much he still loved Georgia. Tears ran down his face when we were in the church and then again at the gravesite. Seeing a big man like that cry quietly made Georgia's funeral more emotional than I expected."

I nodded. "It's good to know Georgia had people who loved her like Jimmy and Pauline. They saw her differently than the rest of the world. I wish I had known the Georgia they knew."

Claudia swallowed hard. "I rarely saw that Georgia myself. Really not until these last few years. I feel like Pauline became friends with Georgia because she felt sorry for her in the beginning. But then, over time, I believe Pauline accepted her and loved her. I think Georgia appreciated that about Pauline. That there was never any judgment."

"Did you know when Georgia approached Rosemary last Saturday, she claimed Pauline wanted her to coordinate the high school reunion?"

Claudia rolled her eyes. "I doubt Pauline would have suggested Georgia take over. The woman had difficulty staying on task. She didn't even keep a job very well or for long. I do wonder why she came to the reunion. When Pauline coordinated these reunions, she reached out to all of us first to help. Georgia never helped, but Sharise and I made ourselves available."

Recalling Sharise's disdain last weekend, I said. "Sharise couldn't stand Georgia because of the way she'd bullied her when they were younger. It may have been a good idea for those two not to be together. Sharise didn't sound like a fan of Georgia last weekend. I don't mean to say this, but if looks could kill..."

Claudia waved her hand. "Sharise is harmless. Besides, I don't think Sharise could avoid Georgia since she's Jimmy's cousin. Sharise and Jimmy are like brother and sister. I believe he confided in her when things were really going downhill with Georgia. Sharise was livid with how Georgia treated Jason. Even I thought Georgia came down on her son too hard. But that was her way."

"Poor boy. Must have been awful to see his parents split. Sounds like he had a lot on his shoulders."

"It's very sad. You know his death was strange too. Georgia didn't want to believe how he died."

"Jimmy mentioned he'd been doing well. Something must have happened for him to turn back to drugs."

"I guess. Georgia had taken Pauline's death hard the year before. Losing Jason made her a recluse. That's why I'm so surprised she showed up at the reunion."

"I wonder what convinced her to attend."

I noticed Claudia's eyes seem to cloud, as if another thought had snatched her away. She blinked. "I guess we will never know. I need to run. It's Saturday, but I'm supposed to work on pulling together some paperwork for Jimmy about his new restaurant. He needs it before going down to Savannah next week."

"Oh, that's exciting. Chicken Shack is one of your clients?"

"My biggest. I remember when Jimmy had the one restaurant. To be honest, I'm ready to retire. I'd like to sell my business within the next year and travel."

"I hear you. Nothing better than being on your own schedule."

"I really hope we can hang out together in the future, Eugeena. Maybe Rosemary will feel better next time."

"Sounds like a plan." I watched Claudia walk away. It occurred to me she didn't walk away quite the way she entered. Her shoulders were down, her gait almost unsteady.

I wondered if our talk had affected her. That certainly wasn't my intention.

I waved to Joss on my way out of the cafe.

Since it was almost lunchtime, I figured it wouldn't hurt to swing by the Chicken Shack and bring home a meal. Save me from having to cook.

My heart almost stopped in my chest when I turned the corner. There were blue and red lights flashing all around the Chicken Shack. My immediate thought.

Oh no, Jimmy!

Chapter 15

The lunch crowd outside the Chicken Shack craned their necks in unison, probably wondering why they couldn't get their favorite chicken meal. With some maneuvering, I managed to make my way up to the front. Yellow crime tape cut me off from stepping forward any further. Even with all the police cars, it wasn't until I saw the tape billowing in the wind that I knew for sure something was very wrong. It didn't surprise me to see Detective Wilkes standing at the entrance.

As if she could sense me amid the crowd, Detective Wilkes turned around and caught me staring. She narrowed her eyes as if she was not pleased to see me.

All these people surrounding me and she would lock her eyes on me.

She started walking towards me, giving me a slight head nod to join her.

Something dropped in the pit of my stomach, making my legs feel like lead. I squeezed past several tall, smelly workers dressed in hard hats. It may have been the middle of October, but the South didn't care about fall weather. It has been an unusually warm day and the caustic body odors about knocked me off my feet.

I blinked my eyes rapidly, tears flooded my eyes as I progressed further away from the smells attacking my nasal passages.

Detective Wilkes appeared concerned as I approached her. "Are you alright?"

"I am, now that I have some fresher air."

She peered behind me, and her mouth curved into a smile before slapping on her serious face. "You're here for lunch?"

I nodded. "I was coming to pick up Amos' favorite chicken meal. I don't deep-fry chicken at home. What's going on?"

The detective opened her mouth and then closed it as if she thought better of spilling the beans.

I reminded her. "You called me over here, young lady." I felt like it was entirely appropriate to remind the detective I was her senior and my schoolteacher voice usually did the trick. Plus, I couldn't get those smells out of my nose and those men were standing at least twenty-five feet away now.

Detective Wilkes sighed deeply. "There's been an incident."

I started to say no kidding but thought better of it.

She was an officer of the law. Though I didn't understand why she wanted to talk to me, I had no intentions of being carted off in handcuffs. I noticed Wilkes looked even more disheveled every time I saw her. Her short hair was sticking up on her head as if she had woken up and kept stepping out the door without looking in the mirror.

Finally, she leaned in. "Everyone else will know shortly since the media is on the scene. This place may not be serving food for a while. The owner has been killed."

I stretched my eyes in disbelief. "No. Jimmy?" I turned to peer behind me, then turned back to the detective. "He's dead. How?"

She waved me away like a fly. "I can't get into the details. Could be a robbery, I don't know yet."

This woman must be exhausted, telling me this information. I felt sorry for her, but the first thing that hit my mind and flew out of my mouth was, "This is really coincidental."

She peered at me. "How so?"

I lifted my shoulders in frustration. "He just buried his ex-wife yesterday. She was killed approximately a week from today." I took a deep breath, realizing my voice was getting louder. I felt a rush of emotions rising from my stomach. "These two people were my classmates. Now we are all not that young anymore, so old age and poor health are factors for us dying. But murder, that's a bit too much to comprehend."

Detective Wilkes nodded. "I'm not ruling anything out. When was the last time you saw him?"

"At Georgia's funeral yesterday. Before that, Rosemary and I stopped in for lunch last week. He was sad about Georgia and told us about her life. She had a lot of recent tragedies, most of it I didn't know."

She looked at me again. "Was this a friendly visit, or were you and Mrs. Gladstone on some mission?"

I eyed her. "What do you mean?"

"Ms. Eugeena, I feel like I kind of know your M.O. Your husband and my dad work together. I know they are actively reaching out to your other classmates with their own investigation. Something I don't approve of, by the way."

"Okay, okay. So we've been asking questions. I think we

should." It was my turn to peer at her more closely. "Why? Do you think us asking questions got Jimmy killed?"

"I don't know, but I agree with you. Something suspicious is going on here. If I were you, I would lie low and not be asking too many questions. You should know from your recent experiences you can run up against the wrong person. I know how much Amos and your family adore you. Anyway, I got to go."

The detective retreated, and I wasn't sure if I should feel angry or scared. Some part of me started feeling PTSD from my last confrontation sneaking up on me. I knew a killer lurked in Sugar Creek. Had he or she struck again? Why Jimmy? It may have been just a robbery, but the timing was way too suspicious for me to handle.

I started my car, not realizing my hands were shaking. Even my knees shook while I drove home.

My phone started ringing before I opened the front door. Once inside, I struggled to find the phone within the folds of my large bag. By the time I pulled it out of my bag, the phone had stopped ringing. Alarm bells rang in my head when I saw who'd left a voicemail.

Rosemary.

For a split second, I feared something had happened to her, but then the phone rang again.

I answered the phone. "Rosemary?"

She breathed into the phone. "Oh my goodness, Eugeena. I had to call you as soon as I found out."

"Rosemary, calm down. Girl, you sound like you are hyperventilating."

"Jimmy. Eugeena, he's been murdered."

"I know."

"What? Did you see the news too?"

"No, I was heading to pick up a meal for Amos and

there were cop cars everywhere. I even ran into Detective Wilkes."

Rosemary said, "Eugeena, he just had the funeral for his Georgia yesterday. What is happening to our classmates?"

"I wish I could answer your question, but I'm just as clueless as you." I didn't want to admit to Rosemary, but I was also scared.

"Do you think this has anything to do with Georgia?"

I hesitated to answer, but something in the back of my mind screamed yes. Instead, I said, "Wilkes doesn't think there's any connection between Jimmy and Georgia's death. At least not yet. Sounds like Jimmy's could be a robbery. But I will say she didn't seem convinced."

"Is there something you know that I should know?" Rosemary asked quietly.

"What do you mean?"

"I know you are privy to details about the investigation."

"That's not true. My family knows information makes me dangerous," I joked.

"Mmm, I also think they would want you to know rather than you trying to find out on your own. Tell me, Eugeena, what should we prepare for?"

"I don't know. Amos told me the detective was leaning toward Jimmy since he and Georgia had some domestic calls on record. In fact, when they left the reunion last Saturday, they had a heated argument outside the hotel."

"You're telling me Jimmy was more likely considered a suspect. With him now dead, do you think the detective is going to be looking at me again?"

"Not if I can help it. There are still some people with way more motive to kill Georgia." At least I hoped that was the case.

No one knew when their time was up. But Jimmy's untimely death had my head spinning.

Was there a killer out there more horrible than anyone could have imagined?

Chapter 16

On Monday morning, I arose earlier than usual. Amos and Porgy had their quality time outside, and now the dog dozed in the living room corner. Amos stood in the kitchen talking on the phone. From what I could hear, they'd finally tracked down the valet from the hotel.

I wasn't sure what they thought the boy could tell them since the argument between Georgia and Jimmy happened over a week ago. Throughout the rest of the weekend, Amos assured me we would still get down to the bottom of these killings.

"I agree with Detective Wilkes," he said. "According to my contacts, the safe was open and empty. It's possible at that time of night while Jimmy had been closing the store, someone hit the restaurant."

"How did he die?" My inquiring mind had been wanting to know since Detective Wilkes didn't spill any of those details.

Amos paused for a minute. "Now don't go getting all upset, but they struck him on the head from the side."

"Somebody hit him over the head like Georgia. And you all are trying to say it's just a robbery because some money was missing."

"That's seems to be the obvious facts."

"Well, I know little about crime, but I would come with a gun to a robbery."

Amos crossed his arm. "I would too. Maybe it was someone who knew Jimmy and didn't intend to hurt him. Instead, the assailant struck him too hard."

"And no weapon has been found?"

"I'm not privy to that information. Detective Wilkes probably is still trying to figure that out. According to the coroner's report, it was a blunt instrument. Probably something readily available in a kitchen. The forensic team has been in that kitchen the entire weekend. I'm not sure if that restaurant will ever be inhabitable again."

I doubted anyone would want to venture back inside the Chicken Shack, which was a shame.

In my opinion, the person who attacked Jimmy appeared to be the same person who attacked Georgia. Usually, if something worked well the first time, it was a safe bet it would work the next time.

I still wasn't able to nail down a time to meet with Sharise. I knew she was probably mourning the loss of her cousin. I was very curious to know what she had to say about Jimmy being killed one week apart from Georgia.

I also wondered if someone had something against the entire family. Their son Jason died last year. Both Jimmy and Claudia had mentioned how well he'd been doing, making the overdose an overwhelming surprise. Now, both his parents had joined him on the other side.

Before I could ponder all the pieces anymore, the phone rang. As soon as I answered, Leesa started talking before I finished saying hello.

"Mama, I hate to do this to you, but I'm at a conference

all day. The daycare called and said Tyric isn't feeling well. Can you pick him up?"

So instead of putting on my snooping hat, I put on my grandma hat instead. When I told Amos where I was going, the grin on his face almost made me mad. We both agreed something fishy was going on, but I knew he wanted me to stay out of trouble.

When I picked up Tyric, the daycare owner practically pushed him out the door. I couldn't blame her, he definitely had the sniffles. I grabbed tissues from my purse and wiped at his nose. It's never a good idea to have sick kids in the daycare.

I felt sorry for Amos and myself, mainly me. I was bound to catch whatever Tyric had. That's the germ game. I had colleagues who stayed sick all the time from teaching the younger grades. I didn't experience it as much teaching eighth grade. But a few experiences with the flu made me remember the importance of self-care, keeping Tamiflu and getting a flu shot.

Poor Tyric started coughing in the car. Once we arrived home, I got him one of his favorites to drink, apple juice, and took his temperature.

"Well, you are not too bad with the temperature, but let's see if we can do something about those sniffles."

Armed with the children's Tylenol cough medicine, Tyric conked out in the bed we kept available for the children. I sat nearby in a chair in the corner so I could monitor his sleeping while perusing the local news station's Facebook page. There was extensive coverage about Jimmy and the Chicken Shack. The reporters repeated the same information Amos had already told me. Everyone called last night's homicide a robbery gone bad.

I sighed and looked up at the big clock on the wall.

Kisha would arrive shortly on the school bus. Sure enough, I peered out the window that faced the front street and watched Kisha's bus approach. I headed outside to meet her and was greeted with a tight hug.

"Girl, you grew a whole inch since the last time I saw you."

She giggled. "I did not."

"Are you sure? You're looking taller to me."

Once inside, we chatted over cookies and milk, our favorite pastime together when she used to be an only child. Tyric woke up from his nap. Now with both children at the table, Porgy left his doggy slumber and sat patiently waiting for crumbs to hit the kitchen floor.

Between two children and a dog, I was grateful for the doorbell ringing. Grandma needed a time out.

I was surprised to see Chris standing at the door. "I didn't know you were coming by to pick up the kids. Are you off work already?"

"Hey, Ms. Eugeena. Yeah, I told Leesa I could swing by to pick up the kids."

"Well, come in. They're both in the kitchen gobbling up cookies. Kisha is wowing us with the day she had at school."

Chris stepped his long legs through the door. He was a tall, imposing man and good-looking. When I first met him, a few years after Tyric was born, I didn't know what to think of him. Over the years I'd gotten to know him; Chris had an intense side but was also a good-natured guy as well. I was sure his career as a law enforcement officer fueled his intensity. I often saw how much he was like Amos when they would get together to chat.

Chris turned to me before heading to the kitchen. "Before I see the kids, I wanted to say I'm sorry about your classmate, or should I say, classmates. Amos mentioned Jimmy, the guy who owned the Chicken Shack, went to school with you, too."

"Yes, it's all very weird. You know you are going to lose classmates anyway as we age, but these two people were..." I peeked around Chris to make sure young ears weren't listening. Then I whispered, "K-i-l-l-e-d. And a week apart. I mentioned this to Detective Wilkes, and she didn't want to say the deaths were related."

Chris nodded. "There's no evidence to say they're connected, but believe me, she's suspicious. There are some similarities."

"Like being knocked on the head. By the way, is she doing alright? I know you're not supposed to gossip about your colleague, but I feel like I know her since her dad is Amos' friend."

He cringed. "I honestly think she's overworked. Wilkes isn't one who usually asks for help. She's all about being solo. I think some of the guys rubbed her the wrong way when she first started. But she has kind of taken me under her wing."

I eyed him. "Has she, Chris? Then you don't need to get yourself in any trouble. She doesn't need to know you know me. That will not make her day nor will it be a good thing for you either."

"I think she admires you. She has mentioned you in the department."

"Mmmm, probably told them to stay clear of the nosy old woman married to Detective Amos Jones."

Chris chuckled. "Wilkes is pretty uptight right now. She was leaning towards Jimmy Hayes being her number one suspect."

"I'm not surprised. So, who is she leaning towards next? Can I ask?"

He stuck his hands in his pocket. "I was going to tell Amos this, but you will eventually find out. The phone records show a text and then a thirty second call from Rosemary's phone."

"She lost that phone. Or better yet, someone took it."

"That's in both of your statements. Someone also took the keys used to access the office."

"That's right." I stared incredulously at Chris. "Someone's setting up Rosemary."

"Pretty scary. On the camera footage, someone is leading Georgia back into the building and down to the offices. I trust you know your friend, but she definitely has made an enemy."

I shook my head. "I appreciate you giving me this information, but don't mess up with Wilkes. It's nice that she's reached out to the new kid on the block."

"Not a problem. I appreciate her taking an interest, but I thought you should know what's going on. Also, one other thing that I heard. Do you know if Rosemary talked to Jimmy at any point last week?"

I frowned, not expecting that. "She and I visited Jimmy at the Chicken Shack last week."

Chris looked at me oddly, as if he wasn't sure I had everything together.

"Is there something I'm missing?"

"Rosemary talked to Jimmy Friday night."

"At the Chicken Shack? She may have gone there to pick up some food, and they started talking. Everyone did that when Jimmy was at the restaurant. He was a talker."

"Okay, that could have been so."

The doubt in Chris' voice set goosebumps on my skin.

Before I could ask another question, the kids came running with Porgy at their heels. Tyric jumped into his dad's arms.

"Hey, little guy. You feeling better?"

Tyric nodded. "Yes."

Chris looked down at Kisha. "How's my girl doing?"

Kisha grinned. "I'm doing good."

My discomfort was forgotten for a few minutes. I really admired how Chris had become a father figure in Kisha's life. Her real dad left the picture when she was still a baby. I hope things worked out for Leesa with Chris. I knew it bothered her being a package deal.

After I watched the kids get strapped in their respective car seats, I waved to Chris. As soon as I saw the taillights, I rushed back inside the house to dial Rosemary's phone.

Rosemary answered on the second ring. "Eugeena, what's wrong?"

I would say a whole lot is wrong.

***

Our conversation turned silent until Rosemary sputtered. "What did you just say?"

"You were seen talking to Jimmy the night he died. I didn't know this."

"I'm sure I wasn't the only person who talked to him. I stopped to get dinner. Michelle called and told me she had to fill in for another nurse's shift. She's been doing that a lot lately, pulling double shifts."

"So, you talked to Jimmy?"

"Yes, you know how Jimmy is... was when he had things on his mind. Well, at least that's how I remembered him."

"What did he want to talk about and how come I had to hear this from a detective?'

Rosemary squealed. "Detective Wilkes told you?"

"No, Chris did. You know he transferred to CPD last month. He's still the new kid on the block, but Wilkes has taken him under her wings. Apparently, she's interested in you again."

"Why, because I talked to a friend? Goodness, Eugeena, the restaurant was full of people and I had Amani with me. I wasn't going to leave my granddaughter at home to go talking with some man, even if he was a good friend. I don't know who's telling folks they seen me without telling the whole truth."

I shook my head, then realized Rosemary couldn't see me on the phone. "Rosemary, this is serious. I've been trying to skirt around the facts, but it's pretty obvious someone is pointing the finger in your direction purposely. Sistah, what are we missing? Are you sure you don't know who this could be?"

"I have no idea, Eugeena. You know me. I go to work, church, and take care of my granddaughter. I lead a simple life. As far as I know, I haven't done anything to anybody."

I held my hand on my forehead. "This is all giving me a headache. Look, that's not all. Apparently, whoever convinced Georgia to return to the hotel had your phone."

Rosemary didn't stay silent this time but yelped as if she'd burned herself.

"Are you okay?"

"Yes. No. Why is this happening to me?" A sniffle, followed soon by heaving.

"Oh, no. Rosemary, don't cry."

Lord, if she starts crying, I'm going to be a puddle too.

"I can't help it," she wailed. "Somebody is setting me up and I don't know why. If Georgia wasn't dead, I would think she did this."

I had to grab some tissues from the box I kept on the

coffee table. "This is something up her alley, but we know she's gone. Now calm down. You have me crying, too. Isn't Amani home from school?"

Rosemary cleared her throat. "Yes, she is in her room."

"Okay, we don't want her to see her grandmother upset. You know that child is an old soul; she'll want to know why you're crying. Don't upset her."

"You're right. Eugeena, I'm scared. I've been trying to walk around with my head in the sand, but this is too much."

"I know. Rosemary, do you remember seeing anybody you knew on Friday?"

"The only person I saw that I knew was Sharise. She worked at the register but kept looking at me. I guess the place was too busy; she never came over to speak. I even waved at her, but maybe she didn't see me."

"I really want to talk to Sharise, but she keeps dodging my calls."

"Really? Do you think she's trying to avoid us?"

"That's a good question. I would like to see how she acts around you. I can reach out to her again to see if we can meet for coffee like I did with Claudia."

When I ended the call with Rosemary, I narrowed my eyes at my phone. Sharise had been avoiding my calls. The first time I called her, she claimed she would get back to me. The second time, I got her voicemail and left a message.

Either she wanted nothing to do with me or she was guilty about something.

I was leaning towards the latter, so I prayed. I had a tendency to be wrong.

Chapter 17

There was something special about the third time. Either Sharise decided it wouldn't hurt to touch base with us or she had grown tired of me bugging her. She returned my call Monday evening, and we agreed to meet around ten o'clock Tuesday morning.

Before I headed to the car, I checked in with Amos in the garage. This morning he was dressed in one of his several pairs of overalls. When he lived next door, I never noticed how many different overalls he had until I saw them hanging in our shared closet. Today's blue denim overalls meant he would ride the lawn mower and trim hedges for several hours.

He not only kept our yard looking sharp, he also mowed the grass next door at the house he still owned. In recent months, he'd been cutting our next-door neighbor's yard too. Louise's longtime gardener had passed and she could use the help.

I joked. "If you don't want to be a private investigator, you can start your own yard service."

He chuckled. "I'm all for whatever can keep me busy. This will probably be the last maintenance for the season.

Everything has slowed down growing. So, you're heading out to see your classmate?"

"Yes. Sharise is Jimmy's cousin. I'm wondering if she will provide more insight into Jimmy's life. I still can't get over that he's dead."

"It's all really strange. I'm not sure if I know how to wrap my head around what Georgia said to Jimmy."

I stared at him. "That's right, y'all found the valet boy. What did he say?"

"Well, he was a bit upset that the woman he saw had turned up dead. Detective Wilkes interviewed him and from what he told her, that was probably why she leaned in Jimmy's direction."

I dropped my bag on the floor and crossed my arms as if to brace myself. "What did the boy say, Amos?"

"The valet said Georgia stepped out of the hotel and plowed into him. She moved so fast she almost knocked him over and she almost fell."

"We saw that on camera. But she turned around and started yelling something at Jimmy."

"Right, the valet got the feeling she hadn't noticed him. He recalled her saying, 'You will get what's coming to you. No one believes me when I tell them things. They all want to say I'm a fool. You are going to be looking like the fool and you will regret it.'"

I frowned. "Looking like a fool and he will regret it. Regret what? Was she predicting his death?"

Amos shook his head. "She seemed to be telling him something was going to happen and that he should believe her. Whatever it was, that's all we got. Jimmy left and went back inside."

"But didn't he say something back to her before he walked off?"

"Yeah, the valet told Detective Wilkes the man told Georgia there were times he wished he never knew her and that she deserved whatever came to her."

"I see. But Jimmy returned to the reunion, for a little while at least."

"We looked at the video over and over. He left a little before the reunion started wrapping up and went out the front door. Never saw him head towards the office area."

"Well, maybe I can get some more information from Sharise."

"Is Rosemary going with you this time?"

"Yes, and we will be at Sugar Creek Cafe. Don't worry, I will be back soon."

"Alright, be careful. We do not know who did this yet."

After starting the car, I waved. While I pulled out of the driveway, dread formed in the pit of my stomach.

From what the valet boy had revealed, both Georgia and Jimmy had practically predicted something bad happening to each other.

Now they were both dead.

***

This time when I walked into Sugar Creek Cafe, one of my students was behind the counter. It was nothing for me to run into a student since I taught for thirty years, but Fay Everett was one of my older students. I taught her when I was about her age now.

"Mrs. Patterson, how are you doing? Or should I call you Mrs. Jones?"

"I opted for Patterson-Jones, but you know you can just call me Eugeena."

"Alright, Ms. Eugeena. It feels weird calling my former teacher by her first name. What will you be having today?"

"I will have coffee with two creams and two Splendas." I

eyed the row of sweets encased in glass. "Do you have any specials today?"

Fay leaned over the counter and pointed to a row of goodies behind a glass panel. "We have sugar-free cinnamon coffee cake."

"That sounds good to me." My quest to lose weight over the years wasn't a secret. I'd lost a considerable amount in the last two years but still struggled with the pounds wanting to make a comeback.

"Eugeena."

I turned around to find Rosemary waving at me.

"I have a table back here," she said. "Sharise is here already."

"Oh, okay." I thought I was early. Rosemary was always ahead of people, but I didn't realize Sharise had beaten me here too. I grabbed my tray and walked to the back.

Rosemary looked like her usual confident self, nothing like the woman who'd been crying on the phone last night.

Sharise looked harried, her eyes swollen. Rosemary and I were pretty shaken about Jimmy's death, but it had to be hard for Sharise losing her cousin.

I'd been thinking about what Sharise said during the reunion when we all had congregated in the restroom.

Someone needs to put her in her place.

I didn't think anything of her statement and probably agreed with her. But Georgia received a permanent placement that same night. That should have never happened.

The killer also had to have some visible animosity against Rosemary. Observing Sharise, I saw nothing more than a woman who came to have coffee with her classmates. There was also nothing on Rosemary's face that reflected any discomfort prior to my arrival. I assumed they'd had a pleasant conversation.

There weren't that many people in the cafe, which was a good thing. We had a few hours before the lunch crowd drifted into the cafe. With Jimmy's death being only three days ago, I had second thoughts about meeting with Sharise. Even though she agreed to meet, the woman was mourning.

Rosemary had selected one of the cafe seating areas that included a long couch. Two side chairs were placed across from the couch. I sat in one chair, immediately feeling comforted by the cushion and curves supporting my frame. "Sharise, how are you doing?"

Sharise sat her coffee on the table between us. "I'm doing as well as I can. It's been really chaotic at the Hayes house."

I took a sip from my coffee, swallowing the warm liquid before talking. "I can imagine. It's all so sudden. I'm really sorry to hear about Jimmy."

Sharise twisted her hands. "Yeah. It's so weird, it could have been me. "

I commented. "I heard it was a robbery."

"Yes, that's what the cops are saying. I was the manager on call but Jimmy decided to close and told me go home."

"Was that unusual?" I asked.

"Yes. He's the CEO; I can't remember the last time he closed a restaurant. He was feeling really down about Georgia on Friday night. I think that's why he showed up at the restaurant. He seemed to want to do something, and he insisted I go home."

I stated, "That's understandable. Some people handle grief by burying themselves in work." I cringed over my choice of words. "No pun intended."

"That was Jimmy's way of handling his stress." Sharise turned up her nose as if she smelled something terrible. "I guess I made it worse. I told him Georgia's death was probably for the best. I argued with him over a dead woman. A woman who never loved him back the way he deserved. She wasn't a great mother either. Those were the things I argued about with my cousin."

I enjoyed the warmth from my coffee, but alarm mixed with the effects of the caffeine. Sharise could have been the last person to see Jimmy alive, and they argued.

I cleared my throat. "I know you and Georgia didn't get along, but was her death really for the best? When I talked to Claudia, she said Pauline's death hit Georgia hard, then she lost Jason."

"That's a lot for anyone," Rosemary said. "Georgia had a way of being spiteful, but we're all human."

"Georgia didn't seem to have sense enough to know she didn't have to make things worse for herself. Sounds like Jimmy tried to help her."

Sharise's face swelled with anger. "Jimmy helped her and gave her chance after chance. He never learned. But I'm glad she finally got what she deserved. And I won't feel guilty. Believe me, we are all better off without her."

The harshness of Sharise's statement had me blinking, but the pure fury in her eyes had me wanting to push my seat back.

I'm not sure this was a good idea!

Chapter 18

I glanced around quickly, noticing Fay had stopped to look at us. She held a cloth in one hand and a tray in the other. I smiled and waved at her. She nodded and moved on to wipe down a table.

Sharise's statement had me swinging my head towards Rosemary. She looked back at me, anxiety in her eyes for the first time. Alarm bells were ringing in my ears and had me clutching my hands in my lap. I faced Sharise. "Guilty?"

Next to me Rosemary stuttered. "You didn't..."

Sharise stared at both of us and deflated before our eyes. With a shudder, she dropped her head in shame. Her voice was so low, I had to strain to hear. "Y'all, you are both looking at me like I killed her."

"Well ..." I stopped, not knowing how to respond. I knew my body felt ready to run even though we were in the cafe, usually a cozy place.

I peered around. We were still the only ones in our area. I spied Fay out of the corner of my eye. She continued to wipe down tables but had moved further away from us. I forced myself to relax my shoulders and face. Sharise had her head bent and her shoulders hunched as if she was in pain. I asked, "Sharise, are you okay?"

Sharise lifted her head slightly, not looking at either of us. Her hands twisted a napkin over and over again. I looked at Rosemary again, who looked stiff as a board. Then I turned to watch pieces of the napkin fall to the table.

Finally, she looked at us. "Jimmy always said my bark was far worse than my bite. When I'm around people who really hurt me, I never retaliate. I may think about it, but I don't have the gumption to do anything. Georgia and I haven't clashed since high school. I was more upset with her over the way she treated Jimmy and Jason. She was a real man hating type of woman sometimes. She could have let Jimmy go a long time ago."

I leaned forward in my seat, hoping to release the tension in my body. "I heard the cops were called a few times on Jimmy and Georgia when they were married. Sounds like they needed to be apart."

Sharise nodded. "That's right. They would get into terrible arguments. Jimmy would get into trouble and people would think that he did something to her, but she was the one who would get violent, slapping and cussing."

"You said Georgia could have let him go a long time ago, but Jimmy stayed on his accord."

"Yeah. It wasn't until Jimmy started dating Florida that he insisted on the divorce. They met like five years ago, and he proposed to her not too long after they started dating. At the time, I thought he was crazy over this younger woman. But I started liking Florida too. She's a lot of fun."

"Still," Rosemary asked, "why do you think he waited so long to get divorced?"

Sharise shook her head, her eyes bright with anger again. "Jimmy really loved Georgia. I don't think he thought it was possible for him to love someone else. He would always say that Georgia didn't have a good upbringing and that she never really knew what love was. I guess he wanted to be the one to show it to her."

I said, "That's admirable. We can't change how a person was raised, but we can pray and love them. People have to learn how to love themselves through a relationship with God."

Sharise shrugged. "We talked about that during our last conversation too. I told him Georgia didn't want to change. Although he felt bad about the way things were left between them, Jimmy agreed that Georgia seemed to be stuck and almost enjoyed her meanness. Funny, he argued with her the last time he saw her."

I recalled the footage Amos had shown me and what they'd learned from the valet. "Did Jimmy say what they argued about before she died?"

"He didn't tell me much. There was something Georgia wanted from Jimmy but he wasn't willing to give it up, I guess. I told him he didn't owe her anything. Then he really got mad with me. That's when he told me to go and that he would close up the restaurant. I tried to apologize, but he didn't want to hear me out. It was like he felt guilty for her dying."

"The cops were looking at him," I mentioned.

Sharise waved her hands. "They were wrong! Jimmy was a big teddy bear. He wouldn't have hurt a fly. If anything, he defended himself against her." She choked, tears streaming down her face. "He was a good man. I don't know what we are all going to do without him. Poor Florida."

Despite my earlier anxieties, I reached over and touched Sharise's hand which trembled. "From all my years of knowing Jimmy, he'd always been a gentle giant."

Sharise took a moment to try to compose herself, her shoulders shaking. "You know what's really a shame? All these years we've been in that location, the Chicken Shack has never had a single robbery."

What?

That had me sitting straight up. "Are you serious? Do you think someone was after Jimmy? With the new restaurants opening, he has been in the news."

Sharise wrinkled her eyebrows as if concentrating really hard. "That's a good point, Eugeena. He was supposed to make an appearance on the Morning News this Friday. Still, I don't think anyone was after him. People loved him, his dad, and *that* chicken. Whoever it was, they hit the safe hard. Cleaned it out! Plus, Jimmy didn't have a predictable schedule. He spent a lot of time traveling from restaurant to restaurant. And like I said, I was supposed to close last Friday night."

I nodded, still absorbing this supposed robbery. In the back of my mind, I knew something wasn't right. Amos confirmed that Jimmy died a similar way to Georgia.

Rosemary spoke up. "When I talked to Jimmy that night, he was planning on going to Savannah the next day. He was so excited about the opening and how the new restaurant looked. I meant to ask him why Savannah."

Sharise nodded. "I think Florida really liked Savannah. She lived there a few years before returning to Charleston. I don't think it ever occurred to him to start a restaurant outside of South Carolina. Anyway, I don't know what will happen. The restaurant has been built, but everything's just kind of on hold for now."

Rosemary suggested. "Maybe Florida will run everything. She is his wife."

Sharise chewed on her bottom lip. "I don't know. She's so broke up over Jimmy. You know she found him the next morning. He hadn't come home so she went looking for him. Anyway, I'm glad you called for coffee again, Eugeena. I hate to say this but I had to get away. I know you've being trying to talk to me, and I want you to know I'm grateful."

I felt bad; I'd called Sharise to do some snooping. Now that we'd talked, I still felt confused. My feelings were so up and down about people these past two weeks I wondered if I had any discernment abilities.

I've been wrong before. But something keeps nagging at me. What am I missing?

Rosemary interrupted my thoughts. "Give Florida our condolences. Eugeena and I both know how it feels to lose a husband."

Rosemary didn't talk about Lawrence that much, but I knew she struggled with his illness.

She grimaced. "At least I had a chance to say goodbye to Lawrence, but the cancer made him so fragile." She took a napkin and wiped her eyes.

I patted her hand. "Yes, a heart attack took Ralph out. But we had some years together and he was able to be around for his first three grandchildren."

This conversation was teetering on the edge of depressing. I found myself wiping my own eyes.

Something occurred to me. "Sharise, do you know if Georgia showed interest in being a part of the business?"

She shook her head. "No, Georgia didn't want anything to do with the Chicken Shack. On one hand she hated it, but she liked the money though. Jimmy gave her money all the time. She didn't even try to keep a job either."

I thought to myself, *That alone was enough reason to hang onto Jimmy.*

"Well, I don't want to hold you anymore. I know there's a lot to do to prepare for Jimmy's funeral."

Rosemary added. "Let us know if you need anything. You and Claudia were a tremendous help planning our forty-fifth reunion."

Sharise wrinkled her nose. "That was all Claudia. She loves to plan and design things. She and Pauline were a duo on planning the class reunions before Pauline died. You know, I'm surprised she didn't take the mantle."

Something occurred to me that Claudia had said during our conversation, but before I voiced it out loud, Rosemary said, "Come on, Sharise, you had some good ideas too. It was you who brought up the idea of getting the Chicken Shack to cater for us."

Sharise nodded. "Florida is really good at the catering thing. She has developed all kinds of items on the menu that complement the chicken. We're called the Chicken Shack, but we are upscale."

I nodded. "I remember her roasted chicken wings. Very nice flavoring. I do hope she can continue the business. The Chicken Shack is so important to the community."

"I hope so too. Jimmy was her first husband, you know. They'd never met if it wasn't for Jason. For a while there I thought Jason liked her, but even he said she was better for his dad."

"Jimmy definitely liked women with state names." I couldn't help but bring it up. This conversation had been too heavy.

Sharise threw her head back and laughed. "Yeah, people

used to tease him about that all the time. But I know he loved Florida. It's a shame they married late in life so they never had children. Jimmy used to joke the business was like their child too. I know he missed Jason though." She pulled her phone out of her purse and peered down. "Ooh, look at the time. Y'all, I need to leave. It was good talking to you both. Florida is struggling trying to get things together for the funeral on Saturday. She asked me to write the obituary. I tried working on it last night but couldn't. After talking to you both I feel like I can write it now."

We watched Sharise gather her things and leave the cafe.

That's when I realized I'd never touched my sugar free cinnamon cake. Feeling ravished from all the emotions, I dug my fork in. The flavors melted on my tongue. Sometimes food felt like medicine, at least it had always been for me.

I looked over at Rosemary, who seemed preoccupied with staring out the window. It was the first time I noticed the window faced the parking lot. A car passed the window and I recognized Sharise's frame. "What are you thinking?"

"I don't know. For a little while there, Sharise scared me. But I don't recall having any disagreements with her. She was pleasant enough to work with during the reunion planning. Did you sense that she had anything against me?"

"No, I didn't. But I can tell she practically hated Georgia, though. You said she was in your office?"

Rosemary looked away. "Yes. I don't know why I didn't think of this before, but the day of the reunion Sharise arrived early and helped me carry some things from my office."

"But she saw where your office was a few times before, right?"

"Yes, but she seemed agitated that day. I don't know, she has her moments. Like last Friday, she kept looking at me but never came over to talk to me." She frowned, "And the committee was all at the same table at the reunion. I barely sat at the table. I was running around."

My eyebrow shot up. "She could could have stolen your keys or phone if you left them on the table."

Rosemary looked around to see if anyone was listening, and then leaned closer to me. "Do you really think we were sitting across from a killer all this time?"

I lowered my own voice. "I don't know. I wish you were there when I talked to Claudia, so I could see how she reacted around you. Claudia was at the table too, right?"

Rosemary nodded; her eyes weary.

I rubbed my forehead. "Something about Claudia seemed off too. Sometimes when I asked her questions, she seemed hesitant to answer."

Rosemary's face grew still. Then, as if she saw something, she visibly shivered. "Could it be both of them? You know Claudia and Sharise didn't return back to the reunion after we talked to them."

I frowned. "How in the world do you know that?"

"Don't you remember? When we left the restroom, they went in the opposite direction toward the elevators."

I sat in awe at how my old brain hadn't remembered that detail all this time. "This Sugar Creek coffee must have all the pistons in our brain firing away. So, they left the reunion not too long after Georgia left?"

Rosemary looked as if she was on the verge of

tears. "I don't remember seeing either of them come back into the ballroom."

I needed to talk to Amos.

And take another look at the hotel footage from the reunion.

Chapter 19

When I got home, the lawnmower was parked in the garage. Amos must have finished with the yard work. He peered at me through the car's windshield and tipped his hat to me, his signal that he would be inside in a few minutes. I was sure he knew I had something to tell him by the look on my face.

As I made my way inside the house, I thought about the first time I looked at the hotel footage. I'd been concentrating on watching Georgia and Jimmy leave the reunion. There was no one else caught on video who'd left the hotel and then returned. Nor did we see anyone else making their way down the hallway towards Rosemary's office.

I knew from when we visited Rosemary's office that the killer probably left through the office exit door. That would have been the cleanest get away without drawing attention. I'd come to the conclusion since the camera hadn't picked up anyone else in that hallway besides Georgia, that the killer used Rosemary's access key to enter the office area from the outside door exclusive to hotel employees.

But who would be that methodical with planning a murder?

I entered the kitchen and checked on Porgy. A bark and patter of paws greeted me from behind, which meant he'd been somewhere else in the house. I suspected our bedroom upstairs. That dog liked to sneak on the bed whenever he had the chance.

Amos eventually joined me in the kitchen. I had taken a pitcher of iced tea out of the refrigerator and poured a glass placing it on the table. I pulled out my notebook to review the list of classmates again. With deep sadness, I crossed Jimmy's name off the list. I could have crossed him off before his untimely death. I never believed he would've killed Georgia.

From our talk with Sharise, the man remained tethered to his ex-wife for years before he found someone new. Thank goodness he'd found a fulfilling love before he left this world.

Amos washed his hands at the kitchen sink and then sat down and guzzled the glass of iced tea. He wiped his forehead with a handkerchief. "How was the meeting with your classmate?"

I gulped down some iced tea myself before responding. "I'm not really sure. Some things she said made Jimmy's death sound odd."

Amos frowned. "There were two different crime scenes, Eugeena. I admit the M.O. seemed similar."

"Yeah, but she said there had never been a robbery in that location. Jimmy's dad opened that restaurant fifty years ago."

Amos shrugged. "Things change, and Jimmy has been on the news lately. People can probably tell that he has prospered with the Chicken Shack. The restaurant business is hard, and they'd branched out into having more than one location in the past five years."

"I thought the same thing. Sharise mentioned she could have been killed, but Jimmy had asked her to leave so he could close up. That was something he hadn't done in years. Doesn't that seem weird?"

Amos thought for a moment. "When people do things out of the ordinary, that could be cause for alarm. But it could have just been fate that he gave Sharise a break. Maybe for old times' sake, he wanted to have the feeling of closing the restaurant since he had become a big boss owner."

I saw what Amos tried to do, but my inner voice felt unconvinced. "Sharise said they argued. She could have been the last person to see Jimmy alive. Believe me, she has a temper. She had me and Rosemary nervous for a minute there."

Amos stared at me. "You said for a minute. Does that mean you think she could have done something to Jimmy?"

I shook my head. "I'm having a hard time with that one. If she was angry enough, yes. I don't have a problem thinking she could have killed Georgia; they really didn't get along. In my conversation with Claudia, Pauline was the glue that held that entire group together."

"So do you think Claudia had a reason to kill Georgia? Didn't you say she worked for Jimmy?"

"Yes, she was his lawyer, but she dealt with his business matters. But here is another theory. Rosemary remembered Sharise and Claudia left the reunion right after we met them in the restroom. Do you remember seeing when they left the hotel?"

Amos shook his head. "No, but I wasn't really paying

attention to them. Let's look back at the video. If they left around the time y'all said, then they shouldn't have been too far behind Georgia and Jimmy."

Amos went down the hall to his office and retrieved his laptop. He pulled up the footage and scrolled through it.

I watched as the screen showed people moving backward in time. "I didn't realize there was this much footage."

"Yeah. Earl did a noble thing supplying us with the video. He couldn't get everything but we got enough information."

I pointed to the footage. "I didn't realize the restrooms were not that far from the elevators."

"These cameras were placed around exits. What do they look like?"

I scooted my chair forward. "Stop, there they are." We watched as Sharise and Claudia entered the elevator. The camera inside the elevator showed Sharise waving her hands like an animated character. I commented, "She really was more upset about Georgia than us. Looks like she was still going on about her." I frowned as I observed Claudia's face. Then watched as she turned to Sharise, her face a mask of anger.

That's interesting. Was she angry with Sharise or about Georgia?

Claudia seemed so calm when I talked to her. But the look on her face chilled me. Sharise appeared stunned.

Amos broke through my thoughts and pointed to Sharise. "She looks scared."

"It looks like Jimmy and Georgia weren't the only ones having a disagreement that night. Something is clearly going on with these two as well."

"Are they good friends?"

I shrugged. "It seems complicated to me. There was this group comprised of Pauline, Georgia, Claudia, and Sharise. Claudia and Sharise worked on the reunion committee for years with Pauline as chair. I feel like the three of them were closer. Pauline seemed to be closer to Georgia than the other two. Claudia tolerated Georgia, but she was cordial. Sharise and Georgia just flat out didn't get along."

Amos shook his head. "My head hurts thinking about the dynamics of that group. That's definitely complicated."

We looked at the elevator opening on the lobby floor.

Amos said, "Only one of them got off and left through the lobby. Where's the other woman?"

"Yeah, Claudia didn't get off. Wait, she got a room that night. Something about she wanted to get away and enjoy the view. If you are up high enough, you can see all the way out to the Charleston Battery."

"That sounds suspicious to me. We are going to have to see if we can track her on one of the floors. There are elevators in the back that she could have come down to access the office area. I may need to reach out to Earl again, but that kind of footage could be gone. They have guests in and out of this hotel so they will not go back almost over a week now." Amos stated.

Claudia or Sharise? I had no clue.

Rosemary brought up the point of both of them being involved. Claudia could have killed Georgia, but I couldn't see why. Sharise could've killed Jimmy in anger, but I also didn't see why a fight over Georgia would push her that far to kill her own family. Was it accidental?

Inside my bag, the phone rang jolting me out of my thoughts. Even though it wasn't evening yet, I looked out the window and noticed dark clouds gathering. It did that this time of year, got darker earlier and earlier.

I dug in my bag for my phone and saw Rosemary's name on the caller ID. "Hey, Rosemary, What's going on?"

"Eugeena, I just saw on Facebook that somebody assaulted Claudia."

I sat up in the kitchen chair and stared at Amos.

Amos asked. "What's wrong?"

"One of my classmates has been attacked. Claudia Benson."

Lord, something is not right here.

Chapter 20

On Wednesday morning, I went to see Claudia at the hospital for myself. I wanted to understand what happened. I'd never worked in the hospital, but for many years, my first husband had been an obstetrician. Years later, Cedric and his wife worked at the same hospital. Between my family of medical doctors and also having taught hundreds of students over the years, I was no stranger at Charleston Medical Center.

I knew where the ICU was located too. A few years ago, my next-door neighbor, Louise Hopkins, had a troubling incident that landed her in ICU.

When I arrived, I wondered if they would let me see Claudia since I wasn't really family. No one appeared to be in the waiting room and with the passing of her husband, I wasn't sure about family.

Now that I was here, I wondered if Sharise had been by. I was still pondering what the two women were talking about in the elevator. I didn't want my mind to go there, but it did anyway.

Did Sharise have something to do with Claudia being in the hospital?

It seemed strange that something happened to

Claudia after we talked to Sharise. But Sharise had nothing negative to say about Claudia that I could remember.

Still, Jimmy was killed after I talked to Claudia. And Claudia had seemed hesitant about something.

Were we stirring up something by having conversations?

One nurse at the desk was someone I taught about ten years ago. Laura Madison was one of my top students, so it did not surprise me to see her with an R.N. on her name tag.

"Hey, Laura, I was hoping to check on my classmate, Claudia Benson."

"Hey, Mrs. Patterson. Are you family?"

I peered around the waiting room. "No, but she doesn't seem to have anyone."

Laura sighed. "You know they brought your classmate in by herself and I've been here most of the morning. I haven't seen anybody. Last night's nurse is a good friend of mine. She did mention there was a woman here, but she didn't stay."

I wondered if that was Sharise. But wouldn't she have stayed with her friend?

"Look, I don't know if you know, but our class has been having some unusual events. You know Jimmy Hayes from the Chicken Shack."

Laura's eyes opened wide. "Oh, wait a minute. You went to school with Jimmy Hayes?"

"Yes, I did. It's horrible what's been happening. A lot of my classmates are scared."

"I don't blame them." Laura frowned. "Didn't someone get murdered at your high school reunion a few weeks ago, too?"

I nodded. "Jimmy's ex-wife, Georgia Hayes."

Laura sucked in a breath and held her hands over her chest. "Oh my! Well, I can tell you someone tried to take your friend out. She got smacked over the head pretty good. It's amazing she's still alive."

A chill ran up my spine. I peered around, wondering if anyone was listening to our conversation. "Is she going to make it?"

"I really shouldn't be talking about a patient with you, but I understand you being upset. Right now, she's in a coma." Laura swallowed. "I guess it wouldn't hurt to have someone in there just in case she wakes up. Poor woman."

I smiled. "Bless you, child! Thank you so much. I promise I won't be long."

When I entered the room, though I'd just heard about her condition, I was not prepared. I stood in the doorway and gulped some air. Claudia looked nothing like the eloquent woman I had talked to a week ago at Sugar Creek Cafe. We were all old. But without her makeup, and apparently, the wig she was wearing, Claudia looked older than her age. Her silver hair was short and cut close to her head. That's when I noticed the big goose egg on her forehead.

Laura mentioned someone had hit her over the head.

Did Claudia see who did this to her? It could have been the same person responsible for Georgia's death and maybe even Jimmy's, too. I peered around the room as if I thought someone was hiding in the corners.

I went up to the bed and whispered. "Claudia, can you hear me?"

I lurched backward in surprise as Claudia's eyes flew open.

"Claudia?"

The woman blinked her eyes rapidly several times

before she looked at me. Her eyes were wide, and she appeared ready to either bolt out of the room or hide under the covers.

"Claudia," I whispered. "It's okay. It's Eugeena. You've been hurt; you're in the hospital."

Her eyes darted around the room and then zoned on my face again. She opened her mouth to say something, but nothing came out.

"You don't have to talk. I can get the nurse for you."

Before I could move a step, she croaked. "Who are you?"

I froze and slowly turned around. "Eugeena. Eugeena Patterson. We went to school together."

She stared at me. "School?"

Oh, no. That bump on the head was really serious. I'd seen this on television but in all my years had never witnessed this. "Do you know who you are?" I inquired.

Claudia's eyes grew even wider than I could have imagined.

I gently touched her arm. "It's okay. Your name is Claudia Benson, and you have a head injury. Let's call your nurse so she can get your doctor."

I located the button on the other side of her bed and pressed it. I turned, expecting the nurse to come sprinting into the room. When I turned back to look at Claudia, her light complexion seemed even paler up close.

Her eyes were frantic as she opened her mouth and shut it repeatedly like a fish gasping for air.

Oh, dear Lord. Help her!

I rushed out of the room to see what was taking the nurse so long but ended up running into a tall figure. I stepped back and lifted my chin, then frowned. "Chris."

Chris stood in front of me and reached out his hand as

if he thought I was about to topple over. "Ms. Eugeena, are you okay?"

"You two know each other?" The incredulous voice of Detective Wilkes spoke from behind Chris.

Before I could respond, Laura, the nurse, came sprinting with another nurse behind her. They went into Claudia's hospital room.

I turned my attention back to the detectives. Then, I noticed something new. Wilkes' shirt was actually tucked into her pants and appeared ironed for a change. Her hair had grown just an inch, so her haircut didn't make her look so much like a fairy from a Disney tale. She'd also brushed her hair and even looked rested. I thought about how I always saw her working alone. Her pairing up with Chris was new. Possibly a good thing.

That was, until she found out he knew me.

I exchanged looks with Chris, who had the look of wanting to be swallowed into the floor. He glanced around the waiting area like something in that direction was more than worth his attention. To save him the trouble of explaining, I spoke up. "Yes, Chris, I mean Detective Black, dates my daughter and they have a son together."

Wilkes glared at Chris. Her eyebrow arched. Then she sighed, as if resigned to the idea. "Why does this not surprise me? I've seen Chris with Amos." She turned her attention to me. "And why were you in Mrs. Benson's room?"

"I was checking to see how she's doing."

Wilkes peeked inside the room. "She's awake. That's good, we need to talk to her."

I stepped back. "Oh, I don't know. I'm no doctor, but I think she has amnesia. The poor woman didn't even know her name and she couldn't remember me. We just talked to each other a week ago. Not to include the fact we went to school together."

Chris asked, "She's one of your classmates too?"

"Yes, she is. I'm afraid this is a bit too much coincidence for me. I hope you are really looking into Jimmy's death a bit more too."

Wilkes frowned. "I admit your class has had entirely too many deaths in the past two weeks, but there was a robbery at the Chicken Shack."

"Are you sure? Did you know the restaurant has never experienced a robbery the entire time it's been open?"

"Well, things change. People are desperate. How do you know that tidbit of information?" Detective Wilkes crossed her arms.

"All you have to do is talk to the employees." I wasn't about to give up my source, although my suspicions about Sharise were returning. She was the only one left on my list.

By the time I returned to my car, I had to call Rosemary and tell her about Claudia's amnesia.

Rosemary stated, "I am not leaving this house. You think she figured out who the killer was?"

I thought about it. The footage of Claudia and Sharise in the elevator. Claudia displayed uncharacteristic anger, and Sharise seemed afraid. I really didn't know these people. They were all acquaintances in high school. Mainly Georgia crossed my path because of her dislike of Rosemary and, of course, later with Ralph dating me.

"It's possible, Rosemary. If so, this reminds me of an episode on a television show where the killer was trying hard to keep from being exposed, killing off people one by one. Except this time, somebody survived."

Now I just needed to make sure in all my

investigating that no other classmates lost their life, including Rosemary and me.

Chapter 21

By Thursday afternoon, I'd gotten restless. In my mind, I wanted to stay in the house too, but that quickly dissolved in twenty-four hours. I needed to reach out to the two people who I could always count on to give me solid advice and insight.

My two aunts were all who remained on my side of the family. Esther was the oldest living member on my father's side of the family. She was cared for by my youngest aunt, who happened to be two years older than me. We grew up like sisters.

I usually visited with them at least once a week when I wasn't too busy. Last night, I realized it'd been about three weeks. Last time I visited, they both encouraged me to attend the reunion.

Before I left, I finished cleaning up the breakfast dishes while Amos sat at the kitchen table. He tapped away at something on his laptop.

"Okay, I'm heading out now."

"I know I don't have to tell you to be careful. I'm really concerned about your classmate who got hit over her head at her house. She's lucky to be alive."

"I thought about it all night."

Amos got up to walk me out. Before I opened the door, he placed his hands on my shoulders and peered down at me. "We will sort this out."

We touched our foreheads together and stayed like that before Porgy barked. We both laughed. Amos grabbed a kiss before saying, "Alright, Porgy, let's go for a ride today."

Usually, he took Porgy when he went fishing. It wasn't the best weather for that today and it seemed like his fishing license would have expired. "Where are you two off to?"

"Joe has some things he's been looking into. I took Porgy over to visit last week with Joe's dog. He recently got a mutt. I figured Porgy could use another canine in his life."

A play date for the dog!

I snickered about that as I drove to my family's home. I needed something to make me laugh. Soon I pulled into a driveway connected to a Pepto Bismol pink house. The color had faded over time, but on this cool crisp fall morning, the house outshined the array of colorful leaves adorning the oak tree in the front yard.

Cora answered the door. "Well, it's about time. We were wondering when you were going to stop by. We heard what's happened."

"You may not know the half of it."

"Oh, no, child. You better come in and tell us. The look on your face has me worried."

A retired nurse, Cora always had to ask. "Are you taking care of yourself?"

I followed her into the living room. "Yes, as best as I can."

"I can't believe about Jimmy Hayes. Didn't his ex-wife get killed the week before?"

"Oh, you and Esther are going to be upset with me."

Cora stopped. "Why? What have you been keeping from us?'

"It wasn't intentional. To be honest, Amos and the kids didn't want me to get involved, but Rosemary Gladstone and I found her."

"You found her body? What is with you, Eugeena, always running across things you have no business?" said a voice from the living room.

I cringed like I was a little girl instead of a grown woman. "Hey, Aunt Esther."

My aunt, in her eighties, looked like a regal queen in her favorite chair. The television played softly in the background, more for white noise. Both Cora and Esther enjoyed reading and were not television watchers.

"Let me explain." I sat down on the couch and explained all that happened. I stopped at my hospital visit with Claudia. Both my aunts appeared shell-shocked and at a loss for words for a change.

Esther finally asked. "You said Jimmy's was a robbery, but you think the same person is doing all of this?"

I nodded. "Especially now since Claudia has been knocked over the head. These folks hung out together as a group in school. Claudia knew all about Jimmy and Georgia's marriage. She and Sharise have an interesting dynamic. Between Pauline's death and losing her son, it sounds like Georgia had a bit of a breakdown. I feel bad about my feelings towards her now that I've heard how bad she had it."

"Well, Eugeena, our enemies are never really other people." Esther sighed, "it says in Ephesians, 'our struggle is not against flesh and blood, but against the rulers, against the authorities, against the powers of this dark world and against the spiritual forces of evil in the heavenly realms.' There are spiritual things beyond us that cause chaos. For some people these forces really work against them."

Cora nodded. "You know what interested me was when you said Georgia stopped going to church. I remember hearing her sing years ago. She had the kind of voice that could move you to tears."

"She did." It suddenly hit me differently about Georgia's loss. God could use any vessel. So many times people get knocked off their paths and never quite get back on.

Esther shook her head. "I remember some of these kids when they came through my class."

"I'm sure you do," I said. "I almost had you for my English teacher."

Cora laughed. "Me too. It was a trip going to school and my sister was a teacher."

"I'm sure my kids thought the same way when I was teaching too," I grinned. I looked at Esther whose face had turned thoughtful. "What do you remember? I went to school most of my life with these folks, but after we graduated, I lost touch with a lot of them."

Esther said, "Yes, the real world reminds you how small the world was in school. Let me see, I remember Jimmy. He was always a big boy, kind of awkward too. Now that I think about it. He always had a crush on Georgia. Georgia was one of those students you don't forget."

"She wasn't a very nice person," I said.

"I remember her being a talker. She had the tendency to talk back which was a real no-no for kids back then. When I was teaching, a teacher would visit a child's home. That doesn't happen these days. Anyway, she was a smart girl, but she wasn't doing her best. I saw why when I visited her house. Her people were dirt poor, and they were a rough bunch. They had a lot of kids in that family."

Esther's revelations further stuck in my gut with how much you never knew a person. "Jimmy ended up arranging his ex-wife's funeral; there was no family. You said she had a lot of siblings."

"Back then, yes. From what I heard over the years, a lot of them met horrible deaths. They were a mean bunch. I remember Georgia being berated by her mother the day I went to visit. She smacked the child in front of me. I told her that wasn't necessary and the woman had the nerve to raise her hand at me. That's why I remember Georgia. She grew up raised by some hellions."

I let all this sink in. There had been a cycle in that family that got passed down. "You know, Amos said there were some domestic calls while Jimmy and Georgia were married."

"Really?" Esther stated. "Jimmy was raised by a gentleman. Jimmy Sr. showed kindness to everyone. He made sure people got taken care of as far as medical bills. He even made sure some kids got scholarships. I can't imagine that his son would turn out any other way."

Cora commented. "But we never really know people. People can be different behind closed doors. Being married to Georgia may have pushed Jimmy over the edge."

Esther nodded. "That's true."

I commented. "In your eighty-two years, you've met many people and seen a lot here in Charleston. Bet you never heard of something like what's been happening to my classmates."

"Child, this is a first. I can see why you would be

suspicious," Esther said. She rocked back and forth like she heard a tune in her head. "Mmm, that man cooked some good chicken. I remember when Jimmy's dad opened the Chicken Shack. Back then, it kind of looked like a shack, not like that fancy restaurant now. The first time I tasted his chicken, I could tell he had the perfect ingredients, flour, good eggs, but I could never figure out the seasoning."

I grinned. "That's the secret recipe. No one knows that."

Esther frowned for a minute. "There was some controversy about that recipe."

I leaned forward. "I never heard about this."

Esther waved her hand. "Oh, this was early on back in sixties when the Chicken Shack first opened. A woman came forward claiming that Jimmy Sr. took the recipe from her. It was real ugly for a while. Apparently, this woman claimed to be his mistress too."

"This sounds like a soap opera." I shook my head.

We all cackled before Esther continued. "People lead messy lives. Sometimes it's hard to clean up those stains. They stick with you."

Being a history buff, I had to know. "Do you remember the person's name? I would love to know how it all resolved. The Chicken Shack is a known tourist spot today. I would imagine they wouldn't want that kind of history coming out."

Esther's glasses had been hanging by a thin gold chain on her chest. She placed them on the edge of her nose. "Let me think. Her name is on the tip of my tongue. I can remember what she looked like, but her name is slipping my mind. Wait, it starts with the letter R. Rolls. Rollins. I just see the last name Rollins. But the woman had an unusual first name too. Give my old mind time to think, Eugeena."

Cora said. "She will get it. Give her time. You just gave her something else to do tonight. So, what's gonna happen to the restaurants? Jimmy built an empire after his dad passed over the first restaurant to him."

I commented. "I don't know. I talked to his cousin Sharise, and she said the grand opening for the Savannah restaurant was on hold. It's possible his wife could run the whole thing."

Cora frowned. "I didn't know he got remarried."

"Me neither. Jimmy never introduced her to me at the reunion. I met her last week at the restaurant. He married a young thing! She's at least twenty years younger than him. Guess what her name is?

"What?" both Esther and Cora asked.

"Florida."

Cora clapped her hands together and threw her head back. "Are you kidding me?"

We all laughed, and it felt good. I always received a release and felt more relaxed after visiting with my aunts.

My phone rang. I look down at the caller ID. "It's Louise, my next-door neighbor. I wonder why she's calling." Amos wasn't at the house. I knew he was out doing something with Joe.

I answered. "Hey, Louise, what's going on?"

"Hey, Eugeena, I had to call you. Something strange is going on." Sounding winded, Louise continued like she was straining. "There's a woman outside your house. She's been parked in front of your house for quite a while. Were you expecting company?"

"No. Are you inside or looking out the window? Are you being safe, Louise?"

"I'm still inside. She can't see me. I'm not going out there. Joss hasn't gotten off her shift yet. You know I keep this front window open for my cats to look out."

We both knew her favorite chair was by that window and she peered out that window more than the cats. Louise patrolled Sugar Creek for years and always knew what was happening before anyone else. She passed the neighborhood watch to me two years ago, which I'd happily passed on to younger neighbors. In the last year, we had a patrol unit that regularly rode through. Amos also had cameras positioned on both properties. Louise followed suit by getting her own camera installed. That didn't stop Louise from sitting by the window.

As Louise continued with her observations, I pulled up the security app on my phone. "I've seen most of your friends and family. This woman is just sitting in her car with the windows rolled up. She keeps turning her head around like she's looking for someone. Anyway, she's making me nervous. I started to call the police but thought I should call you first just in case you have someone waiting for you."

I pressed the button that brought up the camera in front of our house. There was a car parked out front. Something about the car looked familiar to me. "Thank you, Louise. I'll be home in a few minutes. I'm at my aunts' house. Just keep an eye on her. If she does anything crazy, call 9-1-1."

"You know I will."

I disconnected the call and showed the camera footage to my aunts. "As you can see, I got to go. There's a strange woman in front of my house."

Cora stood. "Be careful, Eugeena. Shouldn't you tell Amos?"

"Don't worry, I will."

I rushed towards my car, wondering about this woman and what she wanted from me.

Chapter 22

Sure enough, the car remained parked outside the front of the house. My memory jarred; I'd just seen this car at Sugar Creek Cafe. I gripped the steering wheel once I recognized the person inside.

Sharise stared back at me as I passed her car to pull into my driveway.

This would have been a good time for Amos to be home, but his truck was nowhere in sight.

I cut the engine off and typed him a quick text.

Are you on your way back? I need some help.

Pretty cryptic, but I didn't know what else to say, and Sharise had stepped out of her vehicle and strode towards my car.

Before I opened my car door, I snatched a glance next door.

Thank you, Jesus.

Despite the cool wind blowing today, Louise Hopkins sat bundled in one of her knitted sweaters. Louise had been in this neighborhood long before it became as diverse as it was today. She may have been one of the oldest neighbors, but her blue eyes were sharp and she missed nothing. She was the original neighborhood watch lady.

By the way she watched Sharise approach me, Sharise was fortunate that Louise wasn't one of those shotgun-toting old ladies.

She may not have had a gun, but I knew Louise had her finger handy on the 9-1-1 speed dial button, which she and I both programmed into our phone back before Amos and I were hitched.

I climbed out of my car and threw up my hand towards Louise. "Hey, Ms. Louise."

"Everything okay, Eugeena?" she called out.

Sharise faltered in her steps as she approached, looking back and forth between me and my neighbor.

I addressed Sharise with a tight smile. "I wasn't expecting you. Your arrival made my neighbor a little nervous. We take care of each other around here."

The woman's face crumbled and big crocodile tears flowed. For a minute, I forgot I was being cautious. I had two classmates dead and one laying in the hospital with amnesia. This woman in front of me had a connection to all of them, but I disliked seeing other people cry. I felt tears well up in my own eyes.

Sharise pulled out a wad of tissues and blotted her face. "I'm sorry to invade your privacy. But I didn't know who else to talk to."

Now it would have been courteous of me to invite her into the house, but my senses kicked in when I remembered Sharise had never been to my house. I'd been living here for over thirty years, so looking me up wasn't hard to do. "Okay, what's going on?"

"I went to see Claudia this morning."

"Yeah, I saw her yesterday. Did she get her memory back?" I asked.

Sharise looked at me. "She had amnesia when you saw her too?"

I nodded. "That bump on the head was pretty serious. Who would want to hurt Claudia?"

Sharise shook her head so hard I was afraid she would cause herself whiplash. "I don't know, and I'm scared. She called me and said that she had something to tell me about Jimmy. She didn't want to talk on the phone. I told her I would meet her at her office."

That piqued my interest. "Really? What would Claudia know about Jimmy? Was it about his death? I thought that was a robbery."

"I know. That's why her call was so strange. Anyway, I went to her office. Her car was there, but she never answered the door. "

"You were at her office? Did you see anyone else there? Maybe another car?"

"No," she gulped and stepped forward, lowering her voice. "Eugeena, they think I did something to her. And it doesn't help that I left a voicemail. I was really mad, and you know I have a temper. So I said some things on the phone that I wish I hadn't said. Anyway, the cops were at my door asking me questions like I did something to her."

There was some animosity between these two so-called friends, too.

Okay, I was trying not to judge. I hadn't had the world's greatest track record as a friend. Still, I couldn't help myself. "If she told you she wanted to meet, what made you think she would change her mind?"

Sharise shook her head. "I don't know. Claudia can be wishy-washy. Sometimes she just makes things up. I regret leaving so hastily, but I figured if she heard the doorbell, she would've come. I stood there for almost ten minutes.

I didn't know someone had hurt her. The place was closed up tight. Besides, I had to go. Florida called. She had to talk to the funeral director and didn't want to go by herself."

"What do you think she was going to tell you? Claudia mentioned she was an attorney for the Chicken Shack. Would it have been about the business?"

"I guess. I'm not sure what else it would be about. I'm scared, Eugeena. Something about that reunion went wrong."

"I have to agree. We can only pray that Claudia gets her memory back. She also needs to be protected too. I hope Detective Wilkes has some security around her."

Sharise frowned. "There was a guard outside her door. Do you think we need protection?"

"I honestly don't know." I admitted. "How did you get past the ICU nurse?" Even though I was allowed in, most of those nurses were adamant about sticking to the only family as visitors rule.

Sharise gulped. "I told a fib. I told the nurse I was her sister. We are sisters in a way. I've known Claudia all my life, and she doesn't have any family. She was raised by an aunt who passed a few years ago."

"Well, under the circumstances, Claudia needs support." That's what I said out loud, but in my mind, I wondered if Sharise was telling me the whole truth.

"Jimmy's funeral is in two days, and I've left Florida for too long. I came right over here after I saw Claudia. I needed someone to tell and I don't have anyone else with Jimmy gone and Claudia in the hospital. I couldn't burden Florida."

"It's okay. How did you find me, anyway?"

"The white pages. They're online, you know."

Of course!

"Where will Jimmy's funeral be?"

"At Greater Zion. The Hayes have always been members there."

"I know the church. It's one of the biggest churches here in Charleston. I imagine there will be many people in attendance." I looked up to see Amos's truck flying down the road.

Looks like he received my text.

Sharise's eyes grew wide as Amos swung his truck into the driveway. "Is that your new husband?"

"Yes, it is. You didn't meet him at the reunion?"

"I'm afraid not. For a while, I had to help Florida with the catering. I went to have a good time, but she came short-handed for the reunion."

Amos sauntered over to us and stopped beside me. "Evening, ladies."

"Amos, this is Sharise Hayes, Jimmy's cousin."

Sharise dipped her head like she was doing a formal curtsy. "Nice to meet you. I just wanted to catch up with Eugeena. I will see you on Saturday at the funeral."

"Yes, we will."

Amos and I watched Sharise drive away. We didn't speak until her taillights showed in the distance.

"What was that about?"

"I don't know. The main thing I got from that interesting encounter is Claudia wanted to tell Sharise something before she got clobbered over the head. With her amnesia, we have no idea what she had to say except it was about Jimmy."

Amos raised his eyebrow. "Really? That is interesting."

Very interesting indeed.

Two questions remained. What was Claudia going to share and who didn't want her sharing it?

For all I knew, Sharise could have been covering her crime. Or crimes.

Chapter 23

On Friday night, we were all in our usual spots. Amos had squirreled himself in his office along with Porgy. While the boys were bonding, I sat in my chair with my laptop. I hadn't been on Facebook in a few days. Sometimes it was the only way I could keep up with my family, especially Junior and his kids. My first daughter-in-law, Judy, posted pictures of the twins, who were growing like weeds. The boys had shot up, inheriting their granddad's height.

While I perused Judy's post from this past week, the phone rang. I peered down at the caller ID. "Hey, Cora. Everything alright with y'all?"

"Yes, let me put Esther on the phone. She has something to tell you."

I chuckled. "Alright. I hope I'm not about to get fussed out about something."

"No, not tonight." Esther's throaty laugh came through the phone. "I remembered the woman's name. Dakota Rollins."

"Dakota. That's an unusual name. There's some actress with that name. She was in the movie we saw with Queen Latifah, *The Secret Life of Bees*."

"I remember that movie. That was a good movie, kind

of sad too. Alright, Eugeena. It's past this old woman's bedtime. I'm giving the phone back to Cora."

"Good night, Esther."

Cora came back on, her voice high. "Girl, I just saw on the news about the funeral arrangements for Jimmy Hayes tomorrow. It's going to be at that fancy mega-church, Greater Zion."

"Apparently, the Hayes have been members there all these years."

"Wow, I didn't know. We live in our own worlds. Have a good night, Eugeena. Don't you and Amos be getting into too much trouble."

I guffawed and ended the call. Nothing like family being in your business. I learned snooping from the best. I turned my attention back to my laptop and ventured over to the Chicken Shack Facebook page. A graphic about the funeral services, along with a recent photo of Jimmy, had been posted. Sure enough, condolences had poured in for the slain owner in the comments section. Whoever managed the page replied to or liked every single comment. The post had been shared almost 200 times. 201, after I clicked share.

I kept scrolling not sure what else I expected to see until another post caught my eye.

The founding Chicken Shack restaurant in the Sugar Creek area will re-open and be dedicated in memory of Jimmy Hayes, Jr. on Wednesday, October 21.

I re-read the post thinking that seemed awfully soon. But they had shut the restaurant down for almost a week and Jimmy's funeral was tomorrow. I said out loud, "I'm glad the restaurant will continue to be open. Probably what Jimmy would have wanted."

I clicked around some more until I found Jimmy's

personal Facebook page. Sure enough, there was an outpouring of love on his page as well. I was always curious about the photos people post on their page. I'd heard so much about Georgia and Jimmy's complicated relationship over the past two weeks, I was curious if they socialized on social media.

Jimmy's photo album didn't disappoint and, even though I just ate, it made me hungry all over again. There were all kinds of plates of chicken, people eating chicken, usually with Jimmy standing off to the side grinning.

I scrolled a bit more and found wedding photos of Jimmy and Florida. That one day I saw her, her face glowed, I thought from being in the kitchen. But she was a beautiful woman, glowing in her wedding dress. I felt terrible for her. I wondered why I missed seeing her at the reunion.

I kept going until I stumbled on a group of photos in one post. The largest one showed Jimmy with his arm around a young man who had features that resembled Georgia, but his dad's height. This must be Jason. The post was dated September of last year.

Gone but never forgotten, son. I will miss you.

This must have been around the time of Jason's death. He was a handsome man at one time, but his face looked as old if not older than his father's. Jason's smile was almost a clone of Jimmy's.

The other photos of Jason when he was younger had been shared from Georgia's page. I'd never looked at her page before and realized after clicking, we hadn't been friends on Facebook. She'd shared the photos publicly.

The earliest photo showed him at maybe five or six years old. I remembered seeing him when Georgia attended

Missionary Baptist. He was close in age to Junior and Cedric.

I scrolled to see what else Georgia had shared publicly. It did not surprise me to see most photos were of her, Jimmy, Jason, and Pauline. This was her tribe.

I stopped scrolling. At first, I wasn't sure why.

Now this is an odd photo!

The photo had been taken outside and I could see other people in the background. I knew around July fourth, the Chicken Shack did a big cookout that included fireworks. Barbecue chicken was a part of their menu, but at this event, it was the main course. I attended in the past with my family but had not been in a few years since Amos started having his big fish fry on the fourth.

As I examined the photo, several things popped out at once. Jimmy, Florida, Jason, and Georgia were in the photo. And the date appeared to be last summer before Jason died.

I wasn't expecting a blended family photo.

The only person smiling in the photo was Jimmy. Georgia wore her familiar sour look. Jason held his hand over his stomach and his face appeared pinched. Was he in pain?

On the other side of Jimmy stood his wife. Florida's face held my attention more than the others. When I saw her in person and in the photos, she always smiled, showing off pretty white teeth. This photo was not flattering to her pretty features at all. What could have been a smile resembled a sneer, her eyes were not focused on the person taking the picture but toward Georgia and Jason.

I would say there was some animosity in the photo.

I could see her not liking Georgia, but Jason? I recalled Sharise saying that Jason introduced Florida to his dad.

They wouldn't be together now. Jason and Florida were the same age. Maybe there had been a previous relationship. Who knew?

When I scrolled to the next post, Florida's bright face appeared in a photo with her and Jimmy only. Off to the right stood Georgia, still with a sour look on her face.

She certainly didn't like being replaced.

I had grown tired of Facebook and could feel sleep sneaking into my eyes. I scrolled for a bit more until I came to a video showing Georgia's stricken face frozen in the middle of her speaking.

I clicked play and listened to this immortalized conversation.

They said my boy overdosed. I know he didn't. That coroner even said he had a bump on his head. I'm telling y'all somebody killed my boy. No one believes me. But I know. It all started with that woman.

That had me sitting up, my sleepiness gone.

Killed. Bump on the head. That woman.

Had this all started a year ago? Maybe none of this had anything to do with the reunion.

I examined the post. The video had been recorded a few months ago.

What woman was Georgia talking about? The one thing I knew, Georgia ran her mouth and had never had a problem sharing her opinion.

Everyone said Georgia had become a recluse. She had been beside herself with grief. Aunt Esther mentioned her experience meeting Georgia's family. It explained a lot about her. She must have only felt heard when she turned mean and nasty, the same behavior she saw growing up.

That's when it hit me. I scrolled back up to previous posts until I returned to that odd family photo.

I'd been thinking about classmates all this time, but what person would have had even more reason to hate Georgia. Georgia was the first wife and Jimmy had stayed married to her, even though they had been separated on and off for decades. Then she dragged her feet about consenting to the divorce. That had to be frustrating for a woman who'd never been married and had been waiting for the perfect catch. Though Jimmy was old enough to be her father, with his stature in the community, he was a great catch. And he wasn't hurting for money either.

Sharise mentioned how much Jimmy still loved Georgia. To me, that was clear with him arranging her funeral. That had to sting for the second wife.

Then a really ugly picture formed in my mind.

Amid my pondering, Amos walked into the room. "What are you thinking about so hard?"

I jumped a bit and closed my eyes as if I could stop the assault of theories wrapping around my mind.

"Eugeena, are you okay?" Amos rushed over and touched my arm.

My eyes shot open. "Oh, Amos. I think I know who's behind all of this."

He raised an eyebrow. "You do?"

"I don't know for sure, but when a spouse dies, who has the most to gain?"

Amos looked at me for a moment, then both his eyebrows lifted. "You think? There's no evidence."

"Are we sure? Watch this video of Georgia."

This time, as I heard Georgia's voice, I looked at Amos's reaction.

He turned and looked at me. "What woman?"

"My question too. I'm going to hazard a guess. The

woman that Georgia had the most animosity toward at the moment was Jimmy's wife. Look at this photo."

I showed Amos the blended family photo. "I don't think there was any love between Jason and his father's new wife, either."

Amos shrugged. "Well, you know we had to work some things out with Briana before she accepted you as my wife."

"Exactly. Everyone doesn't work it out like we did, Amos. Now I know I'm just making up scenarios but suppose Jason's death wasn't an overdose. More than likely, Jimmy would have wanted to pass the business to his son like his dad did for him. They tried repeatedly to get Jason clean."

Amos rubbed his head. "So you're saying the motive was to get Jason out of the way?"

I held up my fingers. "It's wild, I know. But I can see animosity against Georgia. Her spiteful behind stood in the way and still was in the way after Jimmy remarried. Two, wouldn't that drive a woman mad to see how much her husband was still involved with his first wife? Claudia said after Jason died, Georgia and Jimmy grew closer. But Jimmy was remarried. And then Claudia got knocked over the head. She's the company's lawyer. Suppose she noticed something in the paperwork and told Jimmy. Maybe Claudia even confronted Florida."

Amos sat down on the arm of the chair. "This is a lot to process. If you came to this conclusion, Detective Wilkes would have too. And she will have evidence. One person can't do all of this without leaving some clues. Let's wait and see what Wilkes finds."

I didn't know if we could wait, but there was still something else I was missing.

Who was Florida Hayes? Where did she come from?

Chapter 24

Greater Zion was the most appropriate location for Jimmy's funeral. Even with a massive sanctuary, the attendees packed inside the church with a number standing around outside. A cold front had snuck in overnight, making it imperative to wear a coat. The ushers hurried to set up metal chairs in the aisle to get more people inside.

This was a very different homegoing than Georgia's funeral two weeks ago, not just because of the mega-church. Jimmy Hayes and his family were well-loved and knitted in the community's fabric as some type of royalty.

When we entered, the front of the church felt a mile away. I could clearly see large portraits of Jimmy, along with rows of flowers surrounding his casket.

The funeral had the most diverse audience I'd ever seen. People from all walks of life were in the pews. Chicken was a common denominator among the races.

One of the more modern churches, Greater Zion had two large screens on either side of the pulpit. The camera panned across the pulpit, showing a few familiar local preachers, including our Pastor Jones, along with several other dignitaries. I remembered watching on the morning news that Charleston's mayor planned to attend. Two senators from the Lowcountry also appeared on the screens as the cameraman continued to pan the audience.

The seats were set up like an auditorium that sloped down towards the pulpit. The Sugar Creek community, home of the first restaurant, was out in force in the middle. As Amos and I walked down the aisle, I glimpsed the Brown sisters, Annie Mae and Willie Mae. My next-door neighbor, Louise, and her granddaughter, Joss, sat further on the other side of the aisle. Rosemary, her daughter, Michelle, and granddaughter, Amani, sat in front of the twins. We squeezed into the row, with me sitting next to Rosemary.

She commented. "This is quite the turnout."

"I expected something like this, but it has exceeded my expectations."

Rosemary asked. "Did you receive a VIP invite to the special memorial service next Wednesday at the Chicken Shack?"

"Yes, an envelope arrived yesterday. I imagine Sharise had something to do with that. I've never been invited to anything VIP before."

I peeked around to see who else I could see. Cora planned to come, but Aunt Esther wasn't doing well. The colder months weren't good for her joints and she preferred to stay bundled. I couldn't blame her. She would have had to be wheeled into this place in her wheelchair which wouldn't have been uncomfortable. Despite the cold outside, the bodies packed inside made the temperature a tad bit muggy.

Amos helped me pull my wool coat off. I watched him

pull out a handkerchief and rub the top of his head, which had grown shiny.

By the time we'd settled in the seats, the choir started singing "We've Come This Far By Faith." I peered around and watched as the Hayes family walked in. Front and center, Florida Hayes appeared to be supported by two young beefy men, one on each side. If the men weren't practically carrying her, the line would have moved at a snail's pace. Florida moved like my Aunt Esther when she could walk.

The widow's ensemble was all black, including a wide-brimmed black hat with netting that covered her face. Florida walked with tentative steps down the aisle as if at any moment she would topple over.

I'd sat with my suspicions from Thursday evening until now, mulling over them. I wanted to reach out to Detective Wilkes, but Amos had warned me it wasn't a good idea. "Let her find the evidence if any exists. You could be barking up the wrong tree," he told me.

Amos had the experience. Besides, now, all I saw was a young woman who suffered a tragic loss. I didn't know her but I knew about loss.

The line of family members entering the church wasn't long but one person was missing.

I leaned over towards Rosemary and whispered. "Did you see Sharise?"

She whispered back; her forehead creased. "No, I would have thought she'd walk in with family. She told us she wrote the obituary. Maybe she's going to speak later."

That made some sense to me but I remained puzzled as the service droned on. Jimmy's funeral may have broken the record for being the longest I'd ever attended. There were a lot of people who eulogized his life, but none of them were Sharise.

At some point, I zoned out from listening and started examining my program. I hadn't read the obituary yet and started reading.

James "Jimmy" Hayes, Jr., 63, was born March 10, 1958, in Charleston County. Son of the late James Hayes, Sr, and the late Selma Jackson Hayes. He departed this life on Saturday, October 10.

Survivors include his beloved wife, Florida Rollins-Hayes.

My eyes focused on that sentence as my mind scrambled. I wasn't sure if I was overheated, but I suddenly didn't feel very well. I closed my eyes, almost afraid to look down at the program again.

Amos nudged me. "Are you dozing? That's my thing to do."

I tried to smile. Amos caught him a nap in church all the time, but this wasn't a smiling matter. At a loss for what to say or do, I shook my head, "I'm okay. It's so warm in here."

Amos patted my hand. "They should have turned the air up with all the bodies in here. It's an unusually cold day, so it's probably throwing the heating system off. Looks like they are getting ready to open the casket for final viewing."

I almost moaned out loud. That was going to take a while, too. Normally, I wouldn't gripe but I could feel sweat popping out under my suit.

What was wrong with me? Maybe I should get some air to clear my head.

As soon as the thought hit me, a wail jolted my tired body awake. I glanced around and noticed other people were doing the same. The wailing appeared to be coming from the front.

From what I could see, several ushers swarmed around where Florida sat. The widow's cries echoed and seemed to ping off the walls.

She hollered "Why?" repeatedly. Grief hit everyone in different ways.

Her pain ran through me like a sharp knife, and I felt like I would faint.

I elbowed Amos. "I think I need to get out of here."

Amos took one look at me and practically hauled me out of the chair. "Your blood sugar level must be low. We shouldn't have skipped lunch."

Oh my goodness. We knew the church would be packed. Since we had a good size breakfast, it didn't bother me. But this long service had dipped later into the afternoon.

I started breathing once we were in the lobby. There were some people standing around, but most seemed to be outside. My mind thought, "It's cold out there. Why would people just be standing around?"

Amos led me over to a bench by one of the tall windows. It may have been cold, but the sun shone bright through the tall windowpanes. I welcomed the warm rays on my face.

"Hold tight. I will see if I can find some juice."

While I waited for Amos to return, I peered outside and noticed the crowd seemed to be looking out towards the parking lot.

I squinted, trying to see. Amos showed up with a cup of juice.

I raised my eyebrow. "Now where did you find that?"

Amos tilted his head back toward the other direction.

"There's a cafeteria back there. They had a juice machine. Drink."

I did as instructed and started feeling better, but I knew I needed to check my glucose. "Can we head out to the car?"

"Sure, I'm all for beating the crowd out of the parking lot."

As we exited the church, I could hear murmurs as Amos and I made our way down the steps.

"Did she do it?"

"I can't believe they arrested her?"

That had me craning my neck. Among the throngs of people, my eagle eye glimpsed familiar red hair and a tall man. Detective Wilkes and Chris stood by a squad car.

"Amos, who's in the police car?"

But before he could tell me, I caught sight of a terrified-looking Sharise Hayes.

No, no, they have the wrong woman.

"You've got to stop Wilkes, Amos. Sharise didn't do any of this."

Amos eyed me. "Eugeena, you can't be sure of that. Apparently, Wilkes found the evidence she needs."

I remembered and snatched open the obituary I'd stuck under my arm. "I know this doesn't make any sense, but we are all missing something here. Read the obituary, that second line." I pointed.

Amos read out loud. "Survivors include his beloved wife, Florida..." He stopped reading and looked at me. "Why are you determined to pin this on her? The obvious person tends to be the spouse, but this is not one of those cases."

"Dakota Rollins."

Amos frowned. "Who's that?"

I bit my lips, knowing I was getting ready to sound even crazier. "Aunt Esther told me early on when the Chicken Shack first opened, there was a controversy over the secret recipe. A woman, someone who Jimmy's dad may or may not have messed with, came forward and claimed the recipe had been stolen. Her name was Dakota Rollins." I stopped babbling. "I wonder what happened to her?"

Amos shook his head. "You're going off the last name over something that happened fifty years ago?"

I shook my head, "Let me call Cora, hold on." I whipped out my phone and dialed the number. Cora picked up on the third ring.

"Eugeena, are you at the funeral? I'm watching this on the news. Did they just arrest someone?"

"Yes, but it's the wrong person. Can you ask Esther if she remembers what Dakota looked like?"

"She might. You know Esther is better with faces than names. In fact, we were on the Facebook page last night when Esther remembered the name."

I frowned. "Were you all looking at anything in particular? Did you run across any pictures of people?"

"Yes, we looked at Georgia's page and we saw Jimmy's new wife. She's a pretty woman too. Jimmy liked his women pretty."

And a little crazy!

"So, Aunt Esther saw the picture of Florida?"

"Hold on, Eugeena."

I waited for Cora to come back on the phone. Amos stood off to the side. The squad car with Sharise was gone, but then I started noticing a swarm of people leaving the parking lot. The funeral services must have finished.

Cora returned. "That's odd. Esther just told me the reason she thought of the woman's name was that Jimmy's wife looks like her. That's silly, that would make her older than us and you said she was younger than us."

Bingo. That's what I needed to know.

"Cora, I'm so glad you called. This is what I needed. I will call back and update you all later."

I turned to find Amos observing me, concern in his eyes. I explained. "Esther mistakenly thought Florida was Dakota Rollins, which makes me think there is a family connection."

Amos peered around as folks continued to mill out of the sanctuary. He stared at me as if I'd grown another head. "Are you trying to say you think Florida is related to the woman who had a dispute over ..." he dropped his voice, "the Chicken Shack recipe. Do you hear what you are saying? I know life can be stranger than fiction. But that's pretty diabolical."

"You think?"

I couldn't prove a thing right now, but I intended to put a stop to this mess.

Chapter 25

The graveside services were private, and with the sheer volume of people who had attended the funeral, that seemed appropriate. That gave me time to do some quick research. I found myself back at Cora and Esther's house, this time with Amos in tow. He still didn't believe me, but I needed him to talk to Esther.

We were in my aunt's living room with iced tea and ham biscuits. Cora must have sensed we were going to be hungry after the funeral, so she had plates set up on the dining room table, buffet style. She even added some potato salad. While we ate, I laid out my thoughts and showed the video Georgia had recorded a few months ago.

Amos sat across from Esther, his eyes wide with the revelations being presented. "So, Florida could be this Dakota Rollins' granddaughter? What happened to Dakota?"

"Good question." I turned to face Esther.

Esther nodded. "I hadn't thought about this in years, but she died. Her daughter found her."

I raised an eyebrow. "Was it a natural death?"

Esther shook her head. "They didn't give the details, but there wasn't any kind of long, drawn-out police investigation that I remember. Of course, this would have been in the late sixties. I can't say they held her death in importance, being a black woman of a certain reputation. Probably most people forgot about what happened. And the Chicken Shack stayed in business all these years."

Amos finished chewing and then took a sip of his iced tea. "So, it's possible there was an investigation, but her death turned into a cold case. That happens more than we like to think with most unsolved cases."

I said. "You know, I looked on the Chicken Shack's Facebook page. The interesting thing about Facebook is since it's been around all these years, it can be the source of a lot of history. Did you know that five years ago the restaurant received a Southeast Outstanding Restaurant award?"

Amos asked me. "Why is that important?"

"Five years ago was when Jimmy started dating Florida. It took her two years to get married to him because Georgia held up the process. I'm wondering if Jimmy being in the spotlight brought him some attention."

Cora waved her hands across her face as if experiencing a heat flash. "He was a good-looking man."

I pointed at her. "That's my point. A real sugar daddy!"

Amos rolled his eyes as Cora and I cackled. Even Aunt Esther grinned as she shook her head.

I needed the breather; my revelations had weighed me down.

"On a serious note, y'all, if someone has it in their mind to get revenge, doesn't it often turn messy? I bet you this woman has been determined to get something back that she thought belonged to her and her family. Going through a court system apparently wasn't something she wanted to do. There are no guarantees. So, what about knocking off the people who stood in her way? I believe Georgia tried to warn or had been warning Jimmy, but he didn't listen."

Amos stated, "This all sounds like the perfect motive for murder or murders, but where's the evidence? That woman today appeared to be a grief-stricken widow."

"Or guilty. I believe she was at all the crime scenes. How she got away, I don't know." I added.

"How do you know she was at all the crime scenes?" Amos inquired.

I leaned forward, placing one finger in the air, "I don't, but she was at the reunion. The Chicken Shack served as the caterer, which was Florida's baby. In fact, Sharise said she had to help her, something about Florida being short-staffed. Where was Florida when she should have been tending to the food? She also worked with Rosemary on other catering opportunities. Most contracts were reviewed and signed in Rosemary's office, so Florida would have been aware of the location. Now why she picked on Rosemary is anyone's guess. Probably because she needed a scapegoat. Maybe she knew Jimmy was a good friend of Rosemary's and that they had history."

I got up and paced like I was some lawyer, specifying all the facts of a case. "Florida could have been at the restaurant. She wasn't the shift manager that night, but she was one of the managers. She had access. Was that safe really that easy to get into? And Jimmy all of a sudden wanted to close the restaurant. Suppose he wanted to ask his wife something but didn't want Sharise around. Maybe Jimmy didn't argue with only Sharise that night. Maybe his wife surprised him. Sharise said Florida found him. What if she was the one who dealt the blow and then put on an act for the police? This is a well-known trick. Wouldn't you say, Amos?"

"Yes, the spouse is usually a suspect and most will pretend to be the grieving spouse."

I continued. "Then, there's Claudia. She was working on some paperwork that Saturday. Maybe she saw something and wanted to talk about it with Jimmy. She could have called Jimmy and left a message since he's always busy. Being his wife, Florida could have found out. Maybe she went to the office in Jimmy's place."

Amos stated. "This all sounds plausible, but I don't know if Wilkes is going to buy this. There's been no evidence of Florida on camera or fingerprints. Unless this woman confesses, and if she's this much of a sociopath, I don't see that happening."

"You're right," I said absently. My mind wandered to what was happening next week. "I have an idea."

Amos, Cora, and Esther, all gave me the look.

Cora jumped ahead of the other two. "You not trying to do something crazy, Eugeena."

I tilted my head to the side. "Of course not, but we need to pray."

I was definitely contemplating something crazy.

And it would involve convincing Detective Wilkes to let Sharise go.

Chapter 26

The city had barricaded the streets around the Chicken Shack in anticipation of a crowd. It was Wednesday morning, the day of the memorial service. The crisp, cool air made the outside event pleasant despite the pending ceremony. It was a fitting way to re-open the beloved restaurant. Someone had already been cooking or had bottled the smell of fried chicken which wafted in the air.

Outside the restaurant, Amos and I sipped steaming black coffee from paper cups. Sugar Creek Cafe served coffee and hot chocolate at a table, along with a few other vendors in the parking lot. The atmosphere floated between being festive and solemn. The community had lost a great soul. Opening his pride and joy was the closest to bringing some normalcy back into a tragic few weeks.

I knew it wasn't quite over yet. A thorough cleanup was in order. That is, if Detective Wilkes did her part. She made no promises to us. Amos and I had visited the station first thing Monday. I presented the same information to Wilkes, who reacted the way I thought she would.

"Ms. Eugeena, I can't just let a suspect go and then

arrest someone else based on old gossip. So what if there is a connection? I can't arrest the woman without hard evidence or a confession."

Basically what Amos said.

By yesterday, Amos managed to track down an old mentor of his, a retired detective now in his eighties. He confirmed there was also an old case for Dakota Rollins. One that had never been solved with some eerily similar circumstances. Someone had bashed Dakota over the head. Now that was too much for me. It made the murders the past two weeks seem like that whole eye for an eye thing.

I hoped Wilkes had gone back to each crime scene with a fresh eye. There had to be some evidence they missed.

While Wilkes and Amos had done their part, I worked on mine. Which was why we were standing out in front of the Chicken Shack this morning with the invitation we received.

Amos had been quiet most of the morning. I shared with him my full plan last night. Even though he drove us to the ceremony, I could sense he was still apprehensive. I nudged him. "You haven't said much since this morning."

He sighed. "What can I say? I know what needs to be done, but I'm not sure there won't be ramifications. If Florida indeed killed all these people, what makes you think she won't retaliate?"

"I doubt she remembers me since we only met that one time. But just in case, this is why I needed to get Wilkes involved. Do you think she believes me now?"

"We're about to find out." Amos gave a head nod toward the person walking towards us.

Wilkes stopped in front of us, her eyes on me and her hand on her hip, like she was preparing for a showdown.

"I've been processing your info for the past two days. There are some coincidences."

I looked over at Amos before responding. "Are there ever really just coincidences? Please tell me you found something."

Wilkes arched an eyebrow. "Our case against Ms. Long is pretty solid. If you think this could help your friend, you could be grasping."

I stepped forward; my voice determined. "But you have the wrong woman. What would be Sharise's motive? What does she have to gain?"

A long sigh left Wilkes' body. Her shoulders sagged as if standing felt like too much effort. "Ms. Eugeena, Ms. Long has more to gain than you think. She's been a part of this family business as long as Mr. Jimmy Hayes, Jr. I have on good word that she is more than likely to have been the one to inherit the business at one time."

Okay, now that surprised me. "I guess that makes sense especially since Jason died. I would think Jimmy really wanted his son to inherit."

Wilkes shook her head. "I agree, but then Mr. Hayes did get married three years ago, so that changed the paperwork. But he was making some new changes before he died. So with all that said I have looked into a few things. Some new questions have arisen, which is why I'm here."

I clapped my hands together. "I know I'm no detective, but y'all have these gut feelings all the time. I believe we're about to find out the true killer."

Wilkes frowned at me. "By the way, I know what you asked from me. How are you planning to do this? You left that out, which has me concerned. This is a highly unusual situation and I'm taking an enormous risk. You are a citizen, even if you are married to a retired homicide detective. Amos, are you good with this?"

Before Amos could respond, a murmur arose in the crowd. A black SUV inched its way down the street. Police deputies made sure people stayed behind the lines until the vehicle pulled into the Chicken Shack parking lot.

We watched as a young man climbed out of the driver's side. He looked familiar to me. Then I realized he had been at the funeral escorting Florida down the aisle.

He moved around to the passenger side and opened the door. Florida stretched her legs out of the door, showing off red high heel pumps. She took the young man's hand before stepping out of the SUV. Dressed in what appeared to be jeans with a loose red top, Florida turned to the crowd, her silky black hair lifted by the wind, caressing her face. Large shades covered her eyes. From where I stood, Mrs. Jimmy Hayes, Jr. looked more like a fashion model.

It occurred to me at that moment, Florida, despite her beauty, had been very subtle about remaining in the background. Now she fluttered to the spotlight with ease. But I didn't discern a butterfly awakening from its cocoon. There was a distinct self-confidence that probably had been there all along. She'd won over Jimmy and infiltrated his business.

Could her motives have been pure? Did she really love Jimmy?

I commented. "She looks different today. Not at all like at the funeral on Saturday."

Amos agreed, his eyes riveted. "She seems to enjoy the crowd too."

Florida waved her hand back and forth like a beauty

queen before stepping inside the side door to the restaurant.

Nope, that was not the same woman wailing this past Saturday.

I turned back to Wilkes, who had been observing Florida Hayes as well. She shook her head. "I've seen some things that strike me as strange. Shall we go inside?"

Amos nodded. "We got this. As long as you hold up your end, Wilkes. You ready, Eugeena?"

"Let's do this."

I prayed as we approached the restaurant's front entrance.

Lord, I'm trusting you that this will go the way it needs.

For this event, certain people had VIP invitations to go inside the restaurant for the ceremony, which was comprised of several pastors, some of the same ones at the funeral. They would pray over the building. I had a feeling Sharise may have had something to do with the list since she was so instrumental in helping with Jimmy's final arrangements. When we stepped inside, I recognized several classmates, including Rosemary. She waved at us. I'd not told Rosemary about my plan. It was best to keep this between Amos, Wilkes, and me.

Especially if something went wrong.

I knew it was the breeze from outside, but I shuddered thinking all of this started three weeks ago at our forty-fifth reunion.

Amos touched my elbow. "We should get a seat."

Someone had placed a podium in the center, and they had pushed the tables and chairs to the side. The local television news stations had placed cameras in front of the podium. That made me pause about the plan, since

I hadn't expected quite this much attention. I turned to Amos. "Can we still do this?"

He looked at me. "When else do you think we can get the opportunity? Besides, she can't hide."

"That's true."

The mayor said a few words about Jimmy and his family's legacy. As the mayor droned on, I observed Florida, who seemed to sit really close to the young man who drove her. That's when I realized I'd seen him someplace else. He was the delivery driver the day Rosemary and I came to visit with Jimmy. Could they just be friends?

I turned my attention back to the podium. My pastor was leading the attendees in prayer. I held my head down as they sent up prayers for the Hayes family, the business and its employees, the community, and finally Florida. After the prayer, the podium remained open until Florida stepped up. She continued to wear her shades even though she was inside.

"Thank you all for attending. Jimmy would have been pleased to see you all here today. I'm sad but overjoyed by your presence. Jimmy loved this restaurant. It was the first, and I want to keep it open for the community."

The media in attendance started spitting out questions, and cameras snapped. Florida threw her hands up to cover her face as she stepped down.

Amos gave me a look as I rose. "Eugeena, you sure about this?"

No! But I wasn't going to say that out loud.

This was my chance to make things right.

***

Sometimes there was some truth in gossip, even though it may get watered down after being passed down from one person to the next. From the moment I saw there was a connection to the past, I felt it in my spirit what Aunt Esther had said last week.

People lead messy lives. Sometimes it's hard to clean up those stains. They stick with you.

Without looking back, I walked over to Florida, who was being helped off the podium by the young man. Her head turned toward me as I approached.

"Florida, I don't know if you remember me. We met about two weeks ago. I'm so sorry about all of this."

She looked at me. "Thank you. I remember you, not your name though. You were here with Rosemary."

I kind of hoped she didn't remember my name. Just some meddlesome old lady, which I was okay with accepting. Being a classroom teacher for thirty years, it was important to always put on a good impression. We met so many new students and parents over the years. I never took for granted the last impression I made on students. I always complimented a student on their strengths.

"Jimmy would have been proud of you. I remembered how much he bragged on you that day when we came to visit a few weeks ago."

Florida attempted to smile, but it came out lopsided. "Jimmy was a good man."

Just a good man. Not the love of your life.

I smiled. "Yes, he was. The best! I'm wondering about another matter. You see, I'm a retired Social Studies teacher and I love history. I recently learned about your grandmother. I'm so sorry."

Florida stuttered. "I don't know what you mean."

"Dakota Rollins. I'd been speaking to the police and thought wouldn't it be good to re-open her case. There's so much they can do with cold cases these days."

Florida formed a thin line with her lips. "That's noble, but the police weren't interested in her case back then. I doubt they would now."

Check. Connection to Dakota Rollins.

"But she was instrumental in the history of the Chicken Shack. She would be proud of you. You're the owner now, right?"

Florida took her shades off. She should have kept them on. Her eyes held no emotion and I had a feeling it wasn't due to grief. It took a certain personality type to kill people and not show any remorse. Often those people were all about their mission and nothing else.

She smiled, showing off bright white teeth. "Those are just rumors."

"Oh, I don't know. There's some truth underneath a rumor. Why else would someone kill her? And it's so sad, someone coming in here doing something similar to Jimmy. He worked so hard to build up the Chicken Shack. It's a little eerie, don't you think?"

Florida exchanged glances with the young man who'd been standing next to her. He stared back at her, looking uncertain.

I believe that young man knows some things.

She turned back to me. "It was nice talking to you again. What was your name again?"

Before I could answer, not that I was planning to remind her of my name, Chris stepped inside the restaurant. He glanced around and then ushered someone else inside. Sharise Long darted inside, her eyes weary and tired, as if she'd been crying for hours.

For a split second, I felt bad about this, but where I'd been suspicious about Sharise before, I now knew she was the key to the whole plan working.

She was the last person standing who hadn't a clue about Florida.

In a few minutes, Sharise was about to find out.

Chapter 27

Despite the number of people in the restaurant, her eyes focused on us. As Sharise made her way over, I could see Amos and Wilkes standing nearby, both giving me the eye.

Florida stretched her eyes wide when Sharise threw her arms around her. "I'm so glad they let me go. I told them they made a mistake. I missed everything, the funeral and the memorial service."

"Why did they let you go?" Florida asked, as if she couldn't believe it.

A mixture of emotions morphed across Sharise' face, first shock and then anger. "I did nothing to Jimmy. I wouldn't hurt anyone, not even Georgia. It was a robbery. Plus, I thought about it. You remember we switched shifts. I was supposed to open and work the next day and you were supposed to close. Oh my goodness, Florida, it could have been you."

The restaurant had grown quiet upon Sharise's arrival. And now angry, her voice went up an octave the more she spoke, drawing even more attention.

Florida had noticed too and appeared like a trapped animal, her eyes darting all around. Her partner had slowly backed away, leaving her standing by herself.

I glanced at Amos and then Wilkes before turning back around. "Sharise, I'm glad the police saw you couldn't have done this. You are an integral part of the Hayes family and part of the Chicken Shack. Girl, even at our reunion, you worked the catering while Florida had to go take care of something else. That's dedication."

Sharise nodded. "Yeah, I did. This place is like home to me. Jimmy and I grew up in this place. I know every inch of it, how the food is made, and I love this community and how they supported us all these years."

Florida curled her lip marring her features. "What are you trying to say, Sharise?"

Sharise looked taken aback. "I'm just telling people that I wouldn't do anything to harm this establishment. It's a family legacy."

In the past, when I tried something new in the classroom, I often improvised to see if something clicked. I'd been doing that this whole time, and what I was about to say next was the biggest gamble. "Jimmy knew how much you loved this place. He loved you like a sister. That's why he was getting with Claudia. Hopefully she will share some good news with you soon as she gets better."

Florida exploded and rammed her finger near Sharise's face. "There's nothing for Claudia to share. This business is mine. Don't think you are going to get any part of it."

There was a collective gasp around the restaurant over Florida's outburst.

Wilkes stepped forward. "Mrs. Benson is still not out of the woods yet with her head injury, but we did find some paperwork for the Chicken Shack. It seems Mr. Hayes planned for his business to be transferred to his son, Jason Hayes. In the event his son preceded him in death, Ms.

Sharise Long and any of her family would inherit the business, making sure it stayed in the Hayes family. When you married Mr. Hayes three years ago, he changed the paperwork to you. But we've found in recent days, Mr. Hayes reverted the paperwork back to Sharise Long. We also found divorce papers in a safety deposit box."

Florida stepped back as if someone had pushed her. "No."

Sharise looked surprise. "But why..." Then Sharise stared at Florida, her mouth open. With a pained voice, she said, "I hate to say this, but Georgia was right about you. I kept telling Jimmy not to pay any attention to what Georgia said, she was just jealous. Maybe Jimmy should have listened to her. He might still be alive right now."

The low murmur in the background rose as conversations increased all around the restaurant.

One media man took it upon himself to move closer with his camera.

Like a well-trained actress, Florida's face crumbled. "Why would you say that? Nothing she said was true. You're not putting this on me."

Sharise yelled. "Jimmy told me. Georgia would not leave him alone. She was convinced you did something to Jason. Georgia said you argued with Jason at the Fourth of July Bash. He'd found something out about you and didn't know how to tell his dad. Then he was found overdosed, but he had that bump on his head." Sharise cried out, "You did this. You killed them all."

I went over to Sharise and put my arm around her. "It's okay, you are going to be okay." I looked at Florida. "Is this what your grandmother would have wanted?"

Florida stared at me. "They murdered her. They

deserved it. All of them. This place existed because of her. This all should be mine."

Wilkes nodded to Chris, who showed up behind Florida. I would bet a bucket of Chicken Shack fried chicken he was in position in case she decided to make a run for it. Out the corner of my eye, I saw two deputies standing by Florida's friend, who now looked like a frightened little boy. I wondered how she got him involved.

"Mrs. Florida Hayes, you are under arrest for the murder of Jason Hayes, Jimmy Hayes, Jr. and Georgia Hayes. You are also under arrest for the attempted murder of Claudia Benson. You have the right to remain silent. Anything you say can be used against you in a court of law."

"No, you can't do this."

We all watched as Florida and her friend were loaded into the back of police vehicles. We didn't know how this was going to turn out, but the world now knew all that had been revealed. There were even more news stations lined up with reporters addressing their cameramen.

There was nothing like word of mouth. Everybody was talking as Amos and I headed back to the car.

"Eugeena."

I heard my name behind me and turned to see Rosemary rushing towards us.

Rosemary huffed from the exertion of trying to catch up with us. "How did you know?"

"I've been doing a little digging. I could have told you about this, but I felt like we needed to expose Florida first. Now that we have, I should ask you about catering that night. Was Florida there?"

Rosemary frowned. "Yes, she arrived early and was

really professional. In fact, she came with that young man. I thought he was the delivery guy."

"He was the delivery guy. I don't know what they will find out about him, but he looked like he would gladly spill. So, was Florida around the entire time?"

Rosemary shook her head. "You know there was one time I looked for her. The table needed to be replenished with more food for the final hour."

Amos asked. "Would this have been after Georgia left?"

Rosemary's eyes stretched. "Yes. And you know what? I started to text her, but that's when I first noticed my phone was missing. I couldn't really look for it, and then I got distracted by something else."

I commented. "I wonder if she kept your phone and badge."

Amos said, "Wilkes and Chris will be on the lookout. The biggest thing that needs to happen is your classmate Claudia needs her memory to return. She may or may not remember what happened, but she might be able to recall what Jimmy's thinking was about changing the paperwork."

"Thank you, Eugeena." Rosemary hugged me. "I'm feeling better now."

"Will you return to the hotel?"

She shook her head. "You know I've been exploring some other things while I've been away from the office. I think I'm ready to do the retirement thing now. There is some good that can come from the bad."

Absolutely!

***

I still had so many questions. Chris came by later that evening to clue me and Amos into what had been revealed during the interrogations. That boy had quickly moved up to be a favorite. I hoped things worked out with him and Leesa. He was one of the good ones.

Chris explained. "Florida's plans weren't as premeditated as they seemed. She had every intention of getting into the Chicken Shack empire but her way was to become involved in the business."

"Was her friend involved?" I asked.

"Samuel? Samuel Webster." Chris told us. "Apparently, Samuel had been a friend of Jason and he'd introduced Florida to him. Samuel claimed he didn't know Florida had an agenda the entire time. He wasn't sure if Florida had anything to do with Jason's death, but his friend had been asking him about Florida. Jason discovered the connection to Dakota Rollins too. He'd been a bit of a history buff himself. It sounded like the argument during the July fourth Bash had to do with Jason questioning Florida's true intentions. Wilkes is still pursuing a lead, but Jason died almost a month later. According to the coroner's report, he did die from an overdose, but he also had a suspicious bump on his head."

I asked. "Could they tell if he gave the drugs to himself?"

Chris nodded his head. "Heroin was his drug of choice, and he had new needle marks among his older ones."

"That's a shame," Amos said. "I'm assuming Wilkes' lead is to try and determine who purchased or supplied him with the drugs."

"Exactly," Chris confirmed. "If Florida had any hand in that, there could be some more suspicions thrown her way."

I asked. "What about Georgia? From Georgia's post she must have known what her son argued about and tried repeatedly to tell Jimmy to be aware of *that woman*. That woman being his new wife."

Chris nodded. "Interesting, Florida did confess she hadn't planned to go after Georgia. She was angry and tired of Jimmy always being there for Georgia. It was her last straw. Your friend, Rosemary just happened to be the scapegoat. Everything from stealing Rosemary's office badge and phone down to bashing Georgia over the head with the paperweight was in the heat of the moment. She threw it all away. She even tried to get Sharise thinking something was going on between Jimmy and Rosemary."

"What? So that explains why the night Rosemary was at the restaurant Sharise kept looking at her talking to Jimmy. She was really trying to set up Rosemary?"

"She definitely was, but then she really messed up," Chris said.

Amos added. "She killed her own husband. That seems premeditated."

"I agree," Chris said. "But Florida claims she hadn't planned to attack Jimmy. Jimmy thought she was on shift. He came in asking about her, but instead found Sharise. He argued with Sharise and told her to go home. What Jimmy and Sharise didn't know was that Florida had been in the restaurant listening to them arguing. Florida had followed him earlier. After the funeral, Jimmy stopped by Claudia's office. Florida knew something was up because his demeanor changed towards her. At first, she thought it was about Georgia's funeral, but it was more than that. Wilkes made Jimmy nervous that he was a suspect, and it got him thinking."

"Anyway, she took care of Jimmy by hitting him over the head with a cast iron skillet. He had his back turned to her so he never saw her coming. She'd washed it off and explained away her fingerprints on the safe due to her being a manager. But it didn't stop her from making some extravagant purchases the next few days. It wasn't so much the purchases, but the timing. She didn't even wait for Jimmy to be buried before she went shopping."

"Wow," Amos and I said at the same time.

We sat in silence for a moment. It was a lot to process.

I finally asked. "So there isn't really much physical evidence, is her statement going to hold up? Why didn't she lawyer up?"

Chris grinned. "She was way too emotional. Ms. Eugeena, you did your thing. I see why Wilkes was okay with you being involved. You got Florida talking and she wouldn't stop. Now she's sitting in a jail cell and she may change her mind later, but we still have a possible witness."

"Claudia," I stated. "What if she gets her memory back?"

Chris nodded. "She's starting to get some memory back, but not of the actual attack. She does remember why Jimmy changed the paperwork. Get this, she claimed Jimmy saw Florida locking lips with Samuel and that's what prompted his suspicions about Georgia's ranting. Georgia had been telling him Florida didn't love him like he thought."

I clapped my hands together. "Well, I'll be. Poor Georgia. That woman had been telling some truth, but her whole demeanor and attitude just put people off."

"It's really sad. The trial for Florida and Samuel has been set for next spring."

"I'm glad; I just hope there are no ramifications for the Chicken Shack. It has a fifty-year history in the community and I hope Jimmy's dream stays alive."

Epilogue

A few days later...

It was a quiet Monday morning, and today, I officially turned sixty-three.

My family, including Junior and his family who returned to Greenville late yesterday afternoon, had assembled at my house on Saturday. I enjoyed the birthday celebration, but I was tired of having a crowd in my home most of the weekend. The events from the entire month had me tired.

No one did any cooking, which was no surprise. Amos came stepping back in with buckets of chicken from the Chicken Shack. They say there is no such thing as bad publicity, and none of the publicity from last week had affected the re-opening of the Sugar Creek restaurant.

Sharise called me last night inviting me to come down to the grand opening of the Savannah restaurant. I told her I'd be happy to attend.

Now that Amos and I were finally alone, we sat and enjoyed the porch. The air was crisp and cool, and we both were bundled in big woolen sweaters. Normally we would have been in the kitchen, but I wanted to relish our time in the rocking chairs. In the south, the temperature could be funny but I was banking on it being cold for a while. There was already a cold front coming in later in the week. When I was younger, I used to wish for snow but always remained disappointed. For now, I was thankful for another birthday. I had some classmates who didn't make it to sixty-three.

I took a sip from the thermos that held coffee with fresh cream and Splenda.

Amos poked my arm. "You okay, you seem pensive today. It's your birthday."

"Just thinking about last week. This entire month. So much has happened. Just to think last month I had no plans to attend my forty-fifth high school reunion."

"Well, looks like it was in the plans for you. You solved the case. You are a pretty good detective."

I grinned and grabbed Amos' hand. "Thank you, Detective Jones. I couldn't do any of this without you. I know you all have been worried about me. I have to admit for a while there, I wasn't okay. I doubted myself the last time and didn't even see the actual killer."

"That's how it is sometimes. I spent decades tracking down killers. Sometimes you have the instinct for the person. Other times you're off. The evidence is all over the place or there isn't any evidence. But you followed that voice inside your head telling you something wasn't right."

"I know where that voice comes from. I couldn't do anything without the Lord placing the challenge before me. I believe He will always equip me to move in the right direction. Although, I have to know when to let Him be in charge."

"Well, you convinced a team of us to help you out with your grand plan. It worked. I believe Detective Wilkes, while she may not say it, has your respect." Amos slipped a thick yellow envelope out of his pocket. "Now that we are alone, I wanted to give you something."

I peered at the envelope. "What's that?"

He smiled. "A little birthday surprise."

I placed my thermos down on the porch floor and took the envelope. Inside was a card. On the front was a big, beautiful cake with lots of candles on it. Above it said, 'For my wife, on her birthday.'

"Amos, you sly man." I opened the card and found a brochure. On the front was a beach resort. "We're going somewhere?"

"It's time we took that honeymoon we never took, don't you think? Sugar Creek will be alright without us while we go have some fun for a change."

"Oh, Amos. When did you have time to plan all this?"

"I had some help from Rosemary. Let's just say we're her first clients."

I started laughing. "Already? That woman didn't waste any time."

Rosemary had decided to officially retire from the hotel and try her hands at running her own travel agency. She told me, "Eugeena, if you are going to be doing this detective work, I can do something interesting during my retirement years too."

Amos leaned over. "So, are you ready to see the world together, Detective Eugeena Patterson-Jones?"

I leaned towards him and planted a kiss on his lips. "I'm ready, Detective Amos Jones."

Let's hope the world is ready for us, because we make a pretty good team.

About the Author

Tyora Moody is the author of **Soul-Searching Mysteries,** which includes cozy mystery, women sleuth mystery, and mystery romance under the Christian Fiction genre. Her books include the Eugeena Patterson Mysteries, Serena Manchester Mysteries, Reed Family Mysteries, and the Victory Gospel Series.

When Tyora isn't working for a literary client, she's either loving on her cats, listening to an audiobook or podcast, binge-watching crime shows or Marvel movies, and of course, thinking about the next book. To contact Tyora about book club discussions, visit her online at **TyoraMoody.com.**

For upcoming releases, **sign-up for her** newsletter (http://eepurl.com/hE3YEz).

Stay tuned for fun posts and upcoming chat dates inside **Tyora Moody's VIP Reading Group** on Facebook (https://www.facebook.com/groups/392249934135315/) .

Books By Tyora Moody

Eugeena Patterson Mysteries
Deep Fried Trouble, #1
Oven Baked Secrets, #2
Lemon Filled Disaster, #3
A Simmering Dilemma, #4
An Unsavory Mess, #5

Reed Family Mysteries
Broken Heart, #1
Troubled Heart, #2
Relentless Heart, #3
Faithful Heart, #4
Wounded Heart, #5

Serena Manchester Mysteries
Hostile Eyewitness, prequel
Bittersweet Motives, #1
Dangerous Confessions, #2

Victory Gospel Series
When Rain Falls, #1
When Memories Fade, #2
When Perfection Fails, #3

An Unsavory Mess